We Kiss Them With Rain

BY FUTHI NTSHINGILA

Catalyst Press
Livermore, California

For further information,
write Catalyst Press, 2941 Kelly Street, Livermore CA 94551
or email info@catalystbookpress.com.

Originally published as
Do Not Go Gentle
by Modjadji Books (South Africa)

FIRST EDITION
10 9 8 7 6 5 4 3 2 1
Printed in Canada

Library of Congress Control Number: 2017947778

Cover design by Karen Vermeulen, Cape Town, South Africa

To children living
on the fringes of society
whose dilemmas are colossal.
Your voices matter.

We Kiss Them With Rain

BY FUTHI NTSHINGILA

We walk amongst the living

We, the departed

We left before our time

We left our young—the children

We died heartbroken

We succumbed to AIDS

We died fighting and angry

We left with many unsaid "I love you's"

We don't rest in Peace

We wander the earth

Wondering about the orphans we left behind

We kiss them with rain

We caress them with gentle wind

We warn them with thunder

We warm them with sunshine

We chase their nightmares with moonlight

We love them with the stars

We, the departed

We walk amongst the living

CHAPTER ONE

After Sipho's funeral, things became progressively worse for Mvelo and her mother Zola. Mvelo was young, but she felt like an old, worn-out shoe of a girl. She was fourteen with the mind of a forty-year-old. She stopped singing. For her mother's sake, she tried very hard to remain optimistic, but hope felt like a slippery fish in her hands.

They had been in this position before, where someone in the pension payout office had decided to discontinue their social grants. One grant was for her being underage, reared by a 31-year-old single mother; the other was for Zola because of her status.

The thought of having no money for food, to live, drove Mvelo mad. "Why are the grants discontinued? My mother is still not well enough to work," she demanded from the official with the bloodshot eyes, who was popping pills like peanuts into her mouth. Her bad weave and make-up made her look like a man playing dress-up. It was obvious to everyone in the queue that the official was hung-over.

"*Hhabe, hhayi bo ngane ndini*, ask someone who cares. You'll see what it says here: DISCONTINUED. You will have to go to Pretoria where all your documents are processed. Now shoo." She waved them away. "It is my lunchtime." The official's mind was on a cold beer to deal with her hangover.

Zola stopped her daughter from engaging the woman any further. "It won't help, Mvelo, let's go back home. We will make a plan."

They were a sad sight. Zola was a shadow of her former athletic self. Her tall frame made her look even worse than she was. People in the queue gossiped behind their hands as usual.

The sight of someone obviously sick seemed to excite them to talk about what was no doubt true for many people waiting there, even if you couldn't see it.

Mvelo and Zola had borrowed money for taxi fare to come to the pension payout hall. Now they would have to walk, and the Durban heat was suffocating. Hot tears stung Mvelo's eyes; the lump in her throat burned. She drank water and began to navigate through the crowd towards the road, heading back with her fragile mother. And just then an unlikely angel in the form of maDlamini materialized from the queue.

"Mvelo," she called out to them.

For once Mvelo was happy to answer maDlamini's call. She nearly fainted from a combination of relief, hunger, and heat. "They said our grants have been discontinued, and now we have no money to get home." Tears of anger and hopelessness about their situation kept coming.

Cooing, maDlamini comforted them and offered to give them the taxi fare they needed. Her act of kindness was fueled by the attention she was getting from the onlookers in the queue.

It was that day, when her mother's disability grant was discontinued, that Mvelo stopped thinking any further than a day ahead. At fourteen, the girl who loved singing and laughing stopped seeing color in the world. It became dull and grey to her. She had to think like an adult to keep her mother alive. She was in a very dark place. One day she woke up and decided that school was not for her. What was the point? Once they discovered that her mother couldn't pay, they would have to chuck her out anyway.

Zola insisted on them going to church even at her weakest. Physically she was weak, but her will to live had not left her. When things got too much, she would say: "Well, what can I say, Mother of God. We, the forgotten ones, we scrounge the dumps for morsels to sustain us through the day to silence the grumbles in our stomachs. We are armed with the ARVs to face the unending duel with that tireless, faceless enemy who has left many of us motherless. We, the forgotten ones, know that rubbish day is on Mondays."

She was not strictly conventional in the ways of the church, though. She prayed differently from other people.

"We come out in our numbers on Monday mornings to scrounge in the black bags that hold a weedy line between life and death for us. We search for scraps to line our intestines, shielding them from the corrosive medicines we have to take, lest we die and leave orphans behind. We dive in with our hands and have no concerns for smells of decay. Maggots explore our warm flesh as we dig into the rubbish to save ourselves, to buy time for our children. We live off the bins of the wealthy. Some of them come to the gate, offering us clean leftovers, while others come out to shoo us away. We are the forgotten ones, shack dwellers at the hem of society, the bane of the suburbs. We move from bin to bin, hopeful for anything to buy us time."

This was Zola's talk with Jesus' Mother at the end of a long hot day, while standing in the middle of the shack that she shared with Mvelo, and washing dishes in a bright blue plastic basin.

"Tomorrow is another day for us," she would say, switching from Mary to Mvelo.

Sometimes Mvelo craved that her mother would just be normal, and wished that she would say "Dear God" at the beginning and "Amen" at the end like other people do. But Mvelo and her mother were not normal, she had come to that realization soon enough.

Mvelo felt sorry for Mary when her mother prayed. Zola didn't believe in the frilly language that most religious people use. She went straight to the matter that was on her mind. She was like Jacob, that ancient man in the Bible, who wrestled with God through the night.

By this time she was not physically strong any more. Even the wind blowing could have pushed her over. But her inner resolve was made of steel. Her inner strength could turn a lion into a gentle purring cat.

After taking her ARVs that she had picked up from the clinic, every evening at eight o'clock on the dot, she would lie down on their single sponge mattress supported by bricks. Mvelo would listen to her mother dream out loud about how she wished that her daughter would one day be a singer. She would get a faraway look about her. In the candlelight, Mvelo would see her eyes shine with the dream of reaching for the stars through her daughter. They would drift off to sleep, lulled by the voices of drunken neighbors, singing, laughing, swearing or fighting, depending on where the mood took them.

Zola's despair was particularly potent on the days when she came back from piece jobs without any food for supper. Even when Mvelo tried to comfort her, by telling her that she wasn't hungry, Zola wouldn't stop blaming herself for their situation. Zola was very sad on those days, and the heaviness that she felt was passed on to Mvelo, who found herself pulled into the darkness of her mother's mood.

But the next day they would start again, with the signs of life pulsating around them once more.

One day the two woke to the buzz of a new church revival

tent that was pitched near their shacks. Loudspeakers and microphones were being tested and prepared for a week of revival. Zola was excited because she thought maybe one of the church leaders would discover her daughter's voice and try to promote her talent. "Start the choruses and give it all you have. Don't hold back, belt it out like your life depends on it," she coached Mvelo before the services. She would only join them after eight because she had to take her ARVs first. Mvelo did as she was told, and each time she sang, she could feel an electric excitement in the tent.

Leaders started asking questions about the young girl with the gift. The replies were always in whispers. "She is the child of Zola. Yes, the one who is sick with the three letters," the fast-talking maDlamini would go on to whoever wanted to listen to the miseries of their lives in the shacks.

Besides insisting that Mvelo attend church every Sunday, Zola also urged her back into joining the girls who went for virginity testing. "Mvelo, I know that you are not doing anything bad with boys, but I want you to go, for my peace of mind," she pleaded with her when she refused. Many mothers encouraged their daughters in this way to ensure that they had not been sexually abused and were keeping quiet about it.

Mvelo relented and went on the testing trips, but it was for survival reasons. She was able to return with a lot of food, hidden in plastic bags, which she collected and saved for Zola. Despite not having enough to eat herself, she was growing and beginning to look like a woman. She had curves in the right places and was tall, but not quite as tall as her mother. A wild flower, growing without proper nurturing, watered by rains and warmed by the rays of the sun, she grew.

Zola's persistent cough grew worse, especially at night. Sometimes deep in the darkness, Mvelo would hear her crying quietly. Those times were accompanied by other heartbreaking sounds as well: a lonely, howling dog seeing restless spirits move about, or crickets calling out, and frogs responding with strange croaking from the swamps. The worst was the mosquitoes, whining for their blood and circling them like vultures. The only night sounds that gave Mvelo hope for the light were the roosters crowing, signaling the approach of morning. Then the wrestling with the night was over. They had lived to see a new day.

They first discovered Mvelo's singing gift when they joined a church after Zola's results came back positive. They had slept very badly the night before because Zola was having trouble breathing, and they both drifted in and out of sleep. Mvelo had to feel out in the dark for her mother to give her water to drink. They did not have enough candles any more. Through the cracks of the shack walls, using moonlight, Mvelo found Zola's bag of pills and got Panados to ease the pain for her.

When the roosters crowed, announcing the dawn of the new day, Mvelo was grateful for the morning light. They got up and went to church where she sang as if the heavens were opening. When she sang, she felt no fear. She drifted into a world where there was no sickness. She sang to free herself from the dank shack they called home, from hunger, from disease and Zola's pain.

Her skin tingled, her eyes closed, and she sang God down into the church. By the time she came to, she was singing alone. The congregation were gazing at her and Zola's face was shining.

"You were no longer with us when you sang like that. I felt a cold shiver down my spine. I swear God was with us. How does it feel to sing like that?" Zola asked her daughter.

The only way Mvelo could explain it was that it felt like she had gone into a trance. "I saw a rainbow of colorful lights flashing in front of my eyes, and when I came to, I felt free and happy."

On their way back home from church, Zola went into a spaza shop and used her last money to buy Oreos. They were her favorite biscuits. Sipho, the man who had been in her life for thirteen years, used to buy them often in their happy times. Zola and Mvelo continued on to their shack, where they sat outside and dunked the Oreos into their tea. In silence, they ate the brown mush with white cream inside, savoring the sweetness, and Mvelo could tell that her mother's mind was far away, remembering the days of abundance at Sipho's house.

Zola chuckled softly as she recalled one of her funny stories. "Do you remember Khanyisile, my friend who worked at Skwiza's *shebeen*? It was around the time when the former white schools started allowing black children to attend." She pinched her nose to mock their Model C accents.

"I think she was named Khanyisile because she was so light skinned. Anyway, she was asked to be a bridesmaid by Skwiza's neighbor, Dudu—the one who married the policeman who ended up using her as a punching bag—and off we went to a salon to have her hair done, to straighten it out from the steel wool of kinky curls.

"Khanyisile sat down on one of those black leather chairs on wheels, with her head tilted back into the basin to wash her hair before the long process to get the desired effect.

"The woman on the chair next to her was having long braids woven into her own hair. She was dressed to the Ts in killer red boots, tight black pants, and an all-eyes-on-my-cleavage cream top. The woman working on her had short plain hair, and her skin was the dark shade that would call the attention of the police who would make her produce her identity document to prove she was not an illegal immigrant. She quietly worked that woman's head like a true professional, separating the long silky pieces and bonding them to the woman's hair with a weapon of a needle. One mistake could lead to permanent brain damage.

"Khanyisile had Vaseline smeared around her forehead to protect it from the burning chemicals. The foul-smelling white stuff was applied to her hair in sections and then she waited for it to untangle her kinks. The indicator of the chemical working was a burning, itchy sensation. After some minutes she waved at her hairdresser to let her know that the burning had started.

"Two teenagers walked into the salon, chatting loudly in their new accents. They said they were going to a classmate's eighteenth birthday party and they wanted to look 'fab' and 'fly' for the occasion. They asked the hairdresser to please do some touch-ups to their peroxided yellowish mops that were meant to be blonde hair."

Zola's attempt at the accent got Mvelo laughing as well. Her hot tea spilled onto her lap, she jumped up, and they roared with laughter some more.

They both wiped away their tears from laughing so hard and Zola continued her story. "So they said their black roots were growing out and they would not like to look like raccoons at the party. The woman who was getting a weave next to Khanyisile could not contain her disgust for what she called the nose brigade. 'These fake Oreos from Model C schools. They walk in here speaking through their noses.' There was an awkward silence as we watched her vent in front of the teenagers. Meanwhile, half her head now had long silky hair, imported from Korea, and the other half was her own short chemically-treated hair.

"Tiny beads of sweat were forming on her face from her

venting. As I looked closer, I saw that this more-African-than-thou woman had a face that was much lighter than her hands and ears. It was obvious she was using a skin lightener.

"The Oreo girls couldn't be bothered by the woman. They sassily chewed their gum and waited their turn.

"By now sniggers were coming from all directions of the salon. As we left, we burst out laughing. I looked at the newly-made-over Khanyisile and said, 'I need an Oreo.'"

Mvelo loved seeing her mother laugh. She didn't do it often any more because she was always thinking and worrying.

CHAPTER TWO

On the last day of the revival, Mvelo was asked to stay behind by Reverend Nhlengethwa. He said he needed to pray for her and to strengthen her with the Holy Spirit so that her gift would grow. In the privacy of his makeshift office, he read from the Bible and placed his hand on her head and prayed. Then he embraced her gently. His kind act reminded her of Sipho, the only father figure she had known. The act brought back all the pain she had had to endure during the past two years. It was a relief to be held. She let her head rest against his broad chest, a sign he took as consent.

What came after was like a bad dream to her.

His hands worked fast, finding what he wanted. He plunged hurriedly and brutally, tearing her world and her illusions to pieces. The eye, her innocence, was gone. Deflowered and destroyed. The thought of a virginity-checker looking at her with disgust distracted her from the burning pain coming from between her legs.

She imagined a pained look of disappointment, shame, and helplessness from Zola, as Reverend Nhlengethwa towered over her with a look of satisfaction while he tidied himself up. He had the smirk of a man content with himself, and did not say a word. The color of life left Mvelo from between her thighs onto the floor. An iceberg of frozen water formed in her chest, freezing her tears and her heart.

She had leaned her head to his chest, and so when he turned from protector to wolf, the shock paralyzed her.

Her soul folded and nestled in a hard shell that formed in her breast. In her mind, she erased her predator from life, sending lightning to suck out all his life force, leaving him as a dried-up lifeless scarecrow in the fields.

She straightened her clothes, wiped away the blood between her legs, and walked home without a word. She put one foot in front of the other until she got home to Zola, whose face was burning with hope. She could not tell her mother what had happened, it would kill her. She was already fragile. "Did he think you can make it in gospel music? Will he put you in touch with Rebecca Malope? Did he—?"

Mvelo's tears cut her off. A dam burst inside of her because her mother's reason for living had been stomped on and trampled over. Through her tears, Mvelo could see her mother's face drop and age from thirty-one to eighty years old.

Mvelo cried for her mother more than for her own pain. She wanted to forget what had happened. She needed the strength to nurse her sickly mother into her grave with dignity. So she smiled through her tears, summoning all the courage she did not have. "No, he just prayed for me. That's all he did. The tent is moving to another town," she said.

They fell asleep silently in each other's arms. It was all they had.

After the tent, Zola lost her ability to speak. She had no energy for it. She just made horrible sounds of pain that came in small weak howls. Mvelo could feel every labored breath Zola took. It was hard work; she would be drenched in sweat just from breathing in and out. Her eyes, although sunken deep into her head, still had a shine when she looked at her daughter, her only reason for living.

Since the revival tent left, Mvelo tried, but she had lost hope, and was withdrawn and sadder than the smell of paraffin and candle-smoke, the smell of poverty. It permeated every piece of clothing and every shack in the informal settlements. She hid the sordid story from Zola, but a mother close to the grave senses things. She knew that something terrible and ferocious had touched her daughter's soul.

From a brick house to this place, Mvelo cried, thinking again of the warmth and safety she had felt in Sipho's house, what felt like a long time ago now. In this forgotten place, girls could not play in the sun in their underwear, splashing each other with water. They had to sleep with one eye open at night. At any point the crude cardboard door could be violently kicked down by night-monsters who, like vampires, were coy to come out into the light.

Uncles. One too many of Mvelo's friends had fallen victim to them. They came and went, leaving behind destroyed lives and broken hearts. They played boyfriend to the struggling single mothers who never seemed to learn; playing house and father to someone else's children bored the uncles. Wolves in sheep's clothes, they turned to the daughters, causing physical damage and a lifetime of mental scars. Mvelo was one of the lucky ones. She was at least able to count Sipho as a father. Though he had let her down, he had never abused her. But through many of her friends and classmates, she knew to be wary of men who called themselves uncles. They could be dangerous.

With these thoughts going round and round in her head, one night it all got too much for Mvelo. She simply gave up any illusion of her mother getting well, and decided to stop giving her the pills. She held her close and said, "Ma, you are not getting better, and we do not have food to help the pills to help you get better. It has become too painful. I have to let you go and I am asking you to let go and rest." She spoke like a woman who had lived many years. She didn't know where it came from.

Zola tried to prop herself up on one elbow and looked her daughter straight in the eye. "Mvelo," she said, "I know something happened to you on that last day of the revival. I can see your stomach is getting bigger and your breasts have lines and color. Promise me you will not do anything to harm the life growing inside you. It is an innocent life. And I will let go on one condition, that you promise you will not allow them to put me in a box. Whatever happens, wrap me in a blanket and send me to God, but please do not let them put me in a box." Her bony fingers were digging into her daughter's wrist. Mvelo promised, even as she didn't know how she would manage to do it.

Zola had always been afraid of closed places. She knew she was being selfish to place this burden on her daughter, asking her to promise something that was going to be difficult. Neither of them had tears; those needed energy they both did not have.

That night they slept without much disturbance. Mvelo was convinced that she would wake up to find Zola gone. But it wasn't to be, she was still laboring on when Mvelo woke up in the morning. Mvelo didn't know whether to be happy or sad.

It was Monday and she went to scrounge around the bins in the suburbs. From one house to another, she would look for anything—glass bottles to sell, dried up bread for her mother. She would take anything that spelled survival. Unlike other beggars, she never rang at gates or looked to make contact. Just their rubbish. She did not want their pity.

For months after Mvelo had stopped giving Zola the pills, she hung on.

The elephant in their shack, Mvelo's belly, grew bigger,

◄———◇———►

revealing the truth of that cruel night in the tent.

Then, one evening, Mvelo herself was struck by a fever that left her delirious. The neighbors found them the next day. Zola, unconscious in a pool of blood she had been coughing up throughout the night. And Mvelo, delirious in a river of sweat from fever. Zola did not make it. The doctors said she died of malnutrition and full-blown AIDS.

At the hospital, when the doctor found life growing inside Mvelo, her eyes were judgmental. She coldly broke the news that Mvelo already knew.

After the harsh words, Mvelo dropped off to sleep.

She dreamed she was being chased by a monster. She was terrified, until she remembered a torch in her pocket. She stopped and faced the creature, beaming the light onto it. Her actions were calm and deliberate. She told herself that she would shine the light onto the beast until she robbed it of its power. It was caught off guard. Now she was no longer the hunted. She was the hunter.

The monster let out a terrified cry and tried to run in the opposite direction, away from the light. She felt sorry for the creature that was now whimpering as she stood over it.

The batteries in her torch were dying, like the monster in front of her. She looked around and realized that everything had become completely still. The only sound was the beating of her heart.

When she woke up, she knew that she would no longer be easy prey. Whatever she decided to do about her baby, it would be her decision. And one way or another, she would carry out her mother's wish of not being buried in a box.

CHAPTER THREE

Mvelo found the perfect person to help her in her mission to free Zola from the coffin. She turned to Cleanman Ndlovu, a dreadlocked Zimbabwean who had made a home among them in the shacks. He had been a teacher in Zimbabwe. Unlike most refugees, he came to South Africa in the early nineties, trying to outrun his pain, only to find hostility in the cities, until he wandered to the shacks where it was possible to get lost among everyone fighting for survival. In these shacks, unlike some places, no one hassled others on the basis of their origins.

Besides, with a surname like Ndlovu, and Ndebele as his mother tongue, he did not stick out. In fact, he fit in more easily than the Xhosas and Basothos who had moved to Durban for a better life. It was his name, Cleanman, which got him teased. He used to help Mvelo with her homework before she dropped out of school.

He held in him horrors of war and secrets that were unspoken. Mvelo told him about Zola's request and the promise she had made to her mother. "But young one," he said, "that is illegal. The municipal laws would not allow such a thing."

"Who cares, Cleanman?" Mvelo was exasperated. "Who cares what the laws have to say? Look where we live, we have nothing. We are thousands here and we share six toilets. Please," she cried, "you have to help me."

He couldn't stand tears. He walked away without giving

her an answer, but she knew that he would help her. He would understand that it is unnatural for a body to be confined in a box.

Cleanman loved poems and he read one at Zola's vigil by a man called Dylan Thomas.

Do not go gentle into that good night,
Old age should burn and rave at close of day;
Rage, rage against the dying of the light—

But she shut him up, maDlamini, the loud mouth of Mkhumbane. "*Wena*, Cleanman," she said, "uZola was not of old age, and she sure wasn't a man. Sit down and stop this English nonsense—"

She was going on but her voice was drowned by the chorus. Women began to sing to disguise the argument. It was the custom of their social graces and discretions to cover any sort of public humiliation or shame. Cleanman looked sad and embarrassed, but he didn't argue. He was not one for public displays or emotional outbursts. He simply closed his thick book, with the dog-eared pages, that had seen better days.

Zola's vigil was beautiful. The whole of Friday night, people came to the shack. Her body was brought back from the mortuary in a simple coffin bought by the neighbors from donations collected in the area. No one listened to Mvelo when she said Zola did not want a coffin. They looked at her with those oh-poor-14-year-old-orphaned-and-pregnant, I-am-glad-I-am-not-you eyes.

Her voice came back at Zola's send off. She sang away her fear about the life that was growing inside her belly, she sang away the dread about digging Zola out of the grave, she sang away the hard road ahead of her as a lonely orphan. She sang until she felt warm inside, like the color orange. She opened her eyes and Cleanman was next to her. "Welcome back, young one, your soul is back in your eyes. It is good to see," he whispered to her. She, too, was released by sending Zola off. She felt free, and was sure that the people who stayed for the vigil had enjoyed themselves. They sang, and one by one they reminisced about Zola.

A woman from the big houses nearby came with a pot of *biriyani*. She looked nervous to be in the shacks, but was determined to speak. She stood up to say a few words about Zola, who used to do washing for her before she became too weak to work. "Zola is someone I will never forget because she blessed my house with a gift that I will treasure forever. My only child, Sunil, could not speak. The doctors thought he was autistic. He stared into space and sometimes he would bang his head on things and scream.

"When Zola came to work for us, he would follow her around. One day I found them sitting and communicating. They had developed their own language. She told me she thought he had speech locked up inside of him. He is now a happy boy who is doing well at school. When I heard about her death, I wanted to come and pay my respects." Ms. Naidoo had intended to drop off the *biriyani*, say a few words, and leave the shacks as soon as possible, but the atmosphere held her there through the vigil.

In her death, Zola had unified people, regardless of their social standing. Neighbors had improvised tins, bricks, and beer cases as seats in front of her shack where they held the vigil.

A nurse from a clinic where Zola had been banned came to pay her respects as well. Mvelo noticed her in the crowd, and thought she was brave to show her face after how she had treated Zola. "It is because of me that she was banned from the clinic," the nurse admitted. "I am burning with shame when I think of it now. I myself am positive, and I had not come to terms with it because it was through my own stupidity, trusting a man that I should not have. When I found out I was positive, I became very angry and I took it out on my patients. Most did not respond to my rudeness. But Zola fought back when I said hurtful things to her. It was my fault, and I want to say, in front of her child here, that I am sorry. I should have been more understanding—"

The nurse was becoming emotional, so the women started singing again.

People Mvelo had never seen before stood up and said things about Zola. It was a beautiful night, the moon was red at first as the sun hid behind it, and later the night turned silver as the moon took over its shift from the sun. Most of the neighbors apologized for gossiping. "*Bantu bomphakathi*, you know me, I just like to talk. Now when I hear you using the Holy Book to rebuke those with loose tongues, I am repenting. I ask you to forgive me," said maDlamini.

One drunk shouted, "*Ya, Mamgobhozi wendawo*," and people chuckled, loudly punctuating her speech. The chuckles encouraged the drunk to get louder, "UmaDlamini, *uNdabazabantu*, Home Affairs, *Ugesi waseLamonti*. There is nothing that she doesn't know under the roofs of these shacks."

Another song rang out to drown the unflattering comments made by the drunk. "Ai, I am just a bored old woman," maDlamini said. "I am sure Zola will forgive me, God rest her soul."

Cleanman looked at Mvelo and nodded. The plan was on. They marked Zola's grave and in the dark they would come back and dig out her coffin and free her into the soil as nature intended. Her coffin was simple and Cleanman watched closely how it closed and opened during the viewing of the body.

Zola had detailed her wishes for what she wanted when

she died. She asked for Skwiza, her only surviving blood relative after Mvelo, to read what she had written. Skwiza stood up—her outfit hugging her tight around her curves softened by age, her eyebrows drawn in that clownish way some women like to do, lips bright red and a sweet perfume that could be smelled all the way from Durban—ignoring the sniggers from the mourners. She was perfect in her delivery, with gestures in the right places, pausing for emphasis where it was needed.

"It is my wish," Zola wrote, "that people should know I died of AIDS. Not a long or a short illness, as they tell us kills most celebrities. Not pneumonia, not TB, not insanity, not witchcraft, but AIDS. This is my gift to all the gossipmongers of Mkhumbane. I give you permission to gossip loudly, not in whispers. Tell whoever cares to know that I lived positively with HIV, and I died of AIDS. Tell them that you heard it from the horse's mouth."

She asked Mvelo to read her favorite passage from the Bible, from 1st Corinthians. "If I speak with the languages of men and of angels, but don't have love, I have become sounding brass, or a clanging cymbal. If I have the gift of prophecy, and know all mysteries and all knowledge; and if I have all faith, so as to remove mountains, but don't have love, I am nothing. If I dole out all my goods to feed the poor, and if I give my body to be burned, but don't have love, it profits me nothing....But now, faith, hope, and love remain—these three," Mvelo concluded. "The greatest of these is love."

Mvelo looked at her mother's face in the coffin. It was peaceful. She would never say another word to her again.

Mvelo imagined that if her mother could say one last thing, it would be, "Sing, Mvelo, you were born to sing." So she did.

CHAPTER FOUR

Mvelo had not known that graveyards were busiest in the dead of the night. When she and Cleanman set out to free Zola from the coffin, the police were chasing and arresting grave diggers who were digging up expensive caskets to resell them to the bereaved. The gunshots rang in her ears. She was terrified and suffocating under Cleanman's sweaty armpit as he shielded her. She had stubbornly refused to stay behind and let him do it alone. She waddled along with her pregnant stomach. Now Cleanman was on top of her, trying to protect her from the gunshots. She couldn't breathe or move.

Then suddenly it was as it should be in a graveyard, dead quiet.

But the silence did not bring her any relief. Instead there was a feeling of approaching doom. She tried to wriggle her nose out of Cleanman's armpit. His body on top of her was becoming heavier. He snored softly against her ear, a sound that would be peaceful and reassuring under normal circumstances, but right now, in the intestines of the night, in a graveyard, his snoring told her she was all alone.

His snores triggered hysteria in her and she began to giggle uncontrollably. The shaking of her body jolted him and he woke up with a start, like a guard caught napping. She pushed him off. "I think they have gone," she said. He had taken vodka to fortify his nerves for the task ahead, but it had made him sleepy instead of brave.

She was wrong. The gravediggers were gone, but the

police were still patrolling. They spotted the two of them as
Cleanman resumed digging up Zola's grave. "*Hheyi*, there are
more. Look over there," a policeman called for back up.

Cleanman knew it was too late to run or do anything, so
he dropped the spade and lifted his hands to surrender. The
vodka drained right out of him and he sobered up. He was in
deep shit. He was an illegal.

Mvelo felt helpless and racked with guilt. She had got him
into this mess. She prayed fervently that they did not realize
that he was not a South African. "It's my fault," she told the
policemen, who were shocked to find a young pregnant girl
in a graveyard at this godless hour.

She told them the whole story about Zola's request.
Cleanman, being Ndebele and with the surname Ndlovu,
spoke the kind of Zulu that is considered proper, similar to the
dialects of the northern regions of KwaZulu-Natal. He asked
the police, "What kind of a man would I be if I could not help
a desperate girl like Mvelo?" His display of respect for the
officers flattered them and softened them immediately.
He even convinced them that in true African culture, "We
really shouldn't be buried in coffins." He gained momentum
when he saw them nodding, and went on to explain that this
business of coffins was an extension of capitalism, a money-
making scheme.

"Just now, my brothers, you were engaged in a gunshot
battle with the owners of these funeral parlors who make a
fortune selling caskets, and then they come back to dig them
up and resell them." There were murmurs of agreement
among the police.

It turned out that two of the three policemen shared the
same surname as Cleanman. On hearing this, Cleanman broke
into a traditional praise song of the Ndlovus, calling out all
izithakazelo, praise-names of the Ndlovus–*Oboya benyathi*,

oGatsheni–thoroughly impressing the men. Of course he gave them his real Ndebele name, Nkosana Ndlovu, instead of the nickname Cleanman, otherwise they would have caught on very quickly that he was from Zimbabwe. If they noticed anything in his accent, they must have chalked it up to the rural areas of KwaZulu.

Cleanman pulled out the half-jack of vodka he had in his pocket. He took a swig and shared it with the policemen. Mvelo knew that he had won them over, but she thought he was going a bit far when he asked them to help him fulfill Zola's last wish by assisting him with finishing the job. She was astounded when one of them went to the security guard at the caretaker's house and came back with three spades. The job took just over an hour to finish.

The humble coffin that Zola was buried in had been uncovered. There was silence. Cleanman looked at Mvelo and said, "Young one, you better walk away. I don't want you to see this. Trust me, I will wrap your mother in this blanket and send her back to God, content."

Mvelo was relieved because she didn't want to see.

The moon was out and the stars were shining. She was at peace and felt that what had just happened must have been with Zola's help.

After the job was done, Cleanman called her back.

"You never saw us, we never saw you. What just happened here never happened at all," said the officer who was not an Ndlovu, looking sternly at Mvelo.

"What just happened here?" asked Cleanman.

The other two broke into a laugh. Then they shook hands with him and drove off.

Mvelo and Cleanman sat by the mound of Zola's grave, where she was now wrapped in a blanket, and offered a last prayer.

At dawn they made their way home, both of them caught up in their own thoughts. The baby was kicking in her stomach, reminding her of the battle that was still ahead. Perhaps because of all the excitement of digging up her mother, the following night she had the kind of pain that made her walk the four corners of her lonely shack until dawn.

When Cleanman came to check on her in the morning, he did not have to ask, he could see her tears. He ran for the wheelbarrow, bundled her onto it, and went towards the taxi rank, but it was a police van patrolling nearby that ended up taking her to King Edward Hospital. The sirens rang all the way from the shacks to François Road. If you want to see a grown man scared, show him a pregnant woman about to give birth with nobody but him there to help her deliver. Cleanman was speechless and shaking. The policeman driving the van put all his weight on the accelerator. The van flew past red robots.

The baby was the last thing Mvelo wanted, but it came and made its presence felt. After ear-splitting screams of pain from Mvelo, Sabekile came out screaming blue murder of her own. Mvelo knew then that the baby had inherited her lungs. The nurse dragged her little kicking legs, and with one hand she shook her slimy body upside down for a while, then put a fat finger inside Sabekile's mouth to pull something out.

Mvelo looked at the snake-like umbilical cord, connecting her to the baby. The ugly memories of that day in the tent came back to her. She tried not to look at the baby, steaming with life, covered in white slime and Mvelo's blood. The nurse snipped off the cord and wrapped the baby in a blanket. Mvelo drifted off to sleep, exhausted, and relieved that the baby was finally out.

She woke up in a panic thinking about what to do with the baby, because she was determined not to subject her to shack life. Then she remembered her dream from when her mother died, and she was calmed. Everything would work itself out.

On the day she was told to leave the hospital with the baby, she went to Manor Gardens, to the house without a wall, and she placed Sabekile there at the front door. At least there she knew Sabekile would have a fighting chance.

She had chosen this house because whenever she came here looking for scraps, the owners never chased her away. It was the only house she had seen in Manor Gardens that didn't have a high wall. It was vulnerable, and yet protected, because the *tsotsis* thought something more dangerous that they couldn't see was on guard, so they didn't take any chances.

"All right, God," she said, fiercely daring him as she walked away, "if you are out there, here is a baby who needs a home where she will grow up without being hungry and where she will be loved. If you can't provide that, then let her die. If you give me just that, I will never ask anything of you again."

Then she willed the baby to live and be found by good people.

She had named the baby Sabekile which means "Frightening," because she knew fear the day a man of God plunged into her shocked body. It felt like an icy hand gripping her heart. It left her shivering, a shivering that got her angry. It made her reckless. But someone with nothing to lose has a chance to arm-wrestle with God, and maybe to win.

CHAPTER FIVE

Zola, in her youth, was a rising star of Hope School in the Valley of a Thousand Hills. She ran like lightning and the school had a proud display of trophies to show for it. Though her given name was Nokuzola, the spectators at competitions shortened her name to Zola—"Zo-la Zo-la Zo-la," they would chant as she approached the finishing line—after Zola Budd who had run in the Olympics.

Nokuzola could not afford running shoes and, like the other Zola, she loved to feel the ground with her feet. She developed a relationship with the grass, or the soil, or the tarmac wherever she was competing. Her feet communicated with the ground. She loved the feeling of her pulse increasing just before the whistle blew to set her and her competitors off.

Her first love was really horseracing. She loved watching the horses, and her greatest wish was to be one of those small men who squat on top of the majestic animals and spur them on to run like the wind. She had never had the chance to be up close to a horse, so she chose to do the next best thing, to run like them. She pretended to be the fastest horse in the race. Her heart would pound and adrenaline would surge through her when she shot from the start to the finishing line, and she felt as light as a feather. As the shouts began, things slowed down in her mind, she would feel the wind pass through her, and a sense of peace would engulf her as she approached the winning point.

One day her rebellious Aunt Skwiza came to visit and told

her about winning a jackpot from betting on a horse named Sweet Apples. After that Zola thought of Sweet Apples each time she raced.

Zola was the pride of her mother, but her father was not happy. He didn't want his daughter wearing those tiny running shorts that he said looked like panties. "It's exposing her body to everyone including perverts, maSosibo, and she is growing," he would protest.

MaSosibo would plead with him, "Just one more year, Baba, and then she will stop. I promise."

He would agree, reluctantly. Secretly he was proud of his daughter, who he thought ran like a possessed mule.

Zola ignored most of the attention coming her way, but she felt compelled to notice Sporo Hadebe. He was unusually dark with a strong jaw and a smile that lit up his face. He was also the most popular soccer player in the school. But it was his unique smell that made her notice him. It was a confusing smell that wasn't a perfume or sweat from practice, but emanated from him alone.

She knew when he was approaching before she saw him appearing around corners, or when he had entered the classroom. Her new interest in Sporo drew her to the game of soccer, just to watch him play.

Her eyes zoomed in and took him in, section by section. She noticed his perfectly toned calves, and that his right leg was slightly crooked at the knee, giving him a unique run. The muscles in his thighs separated like the pictures in a biology book. When the boys took off their T-shirts after practice, she saw that each muscle on his stomach was sculpted, with not an ounce of fat in sight. His arms were strong, and when he smiled, dimples revealed themselves on his cheeks. Could this boy be any more beautiful and unaware of it than he was? She would try not to stare, but failed completely.

←———◇———→

At first Zola thought she was dreaming when Sporo made advances towards her. Not only was he fast on his feet, he was also smart in class and funny too. But despite all of this, he was not arrogant. Zola had promised herself that she would stay away from boys as it was a matter of life and death if her strict father found out. But she couldn't do that with Sporo. There was a sense of urgency in her.

They talked after PE classes and on trips to and from school during athletics competitions. She even began to follow soccer, which pleased and puzzled her father. They made quite a pair, Zola and Sporo. The envious ones looked on with contempt, while others openly admired the two. They became inseparable, and were very sweet together. Even the teaching staff looked the other way from this budding romance instead of reprimanding them like they would usually do. "They seem mature enough to be responsible," said the life skills teacher, Pearl, who took an interest in the lives of her students.

"If you say so. Just don't forget that these are teenagers with raging hormones," said Mr. Zondo, the English teacher, who objected mostly because he couldn't stop thinking about Zola himself. The thought of her with someone else turned him into a jealous schoolboy.

Mr. Zondo would sit by the window and watch her during lunch breaks. He hated it when he saw her laughing at one of Sporo's jokes. As much as he loved soccer, he began to hate Sporo's easy manner. He hated how Sporo put his arm around Zola's shoulders, and the way he looked at her, the confidences they obviously shared. He knew the day Zola lost her virginity to Sporo.

She began falling apart, not submitting homework, and her running slowed, ever so slightly at first, until the day she fainted in the field. Mr. Zondo wanted to scream out loud like somebody had broken his heart. "You know, now that I think about it, it's not even that I was in love with that girl. A part of me wanted to just preserve her and keep her out of harm's way," he confided to shell-shocked Pearl.

Zola had confessed her private fears to Pearl, who had listened with a combination of sympathy and relief. She had her eyes set on Mr. Zondo, who seemed to have his set on Zola, who had hers firmly on Sporo. Pearl was relieved to hear that the girl had no interest in Mr. Zondo. Instead, she was terrified that she could be pregnant from her liaison with Sporo, and that she would surely be killed by her father. This meant that Mr. Zondo would be Pearl's when he realized that the girl had no interest in him. Pearl bought a pregnancy test and asked Zola to pee on the stick so that the line could confirm if she was or not.

Pearl comforted the girl the best she knew how when the line came out pink. Zola cried until she had no more tears left. Pearl made motherly sounds. "There there, Zola, it is not the end of the world. You will live through this difficult time. Do you want me to speak to your mother, or would you prefer to tell her yourself?"

This question brought more tears to Zola's eyes. It stung her back to the new realities she had to face. She didn't know how she was going to face her parents. "No no no, please. I will speak to them myself," she told Pearl.

But first she had to tell Sporo, and they would decide what to do. The thought of having him by her side gave her hope. She would not be alone. It gave her the strength to get through the weekend at home.

On Monday at lunchtime, she and Sporo sat under their tree. She was more quiet than usual. Sporo was puzzled, but he was his usual cool self.

"Sporo, I fainted at practice on Friday," she said finally. "Teacher Pearl and I talked about us, you know, what we did." She paused and searched his face.

He simply smiled and nodded.

"Well, we did a test, Sporo, and it confirmed that I am pregnant." She looked at him closely, trying to gauge his reaction.

Again just a smile, which sent her into a new wave of panic.

"Sporo, this is not a joke. My father is going to kill me, and probably you too." Her voice was shaking.

"He won't, you are his child. He will calm down in time. You'll see. And if the baby is a boy, he will be a soccer player, and if it is a girl she will be beautiful like you." His response did not surprise Zola, but it did nothing to alleviate her anxiety.

He was the kind of boy who never seemed to be rattled by anything. Even the righteous fury of Zola's father didn't scare him. "Look, I can leave school and find work so I can look after you. I will tell my parents to come and speak to your parents. If they throw you out, Zola, I would be very happy for you to live at our home." He was getting carried away with his elaborate plans.

"Hang on," said Zola, catching her breath. "I haven't told my parents anything yet. We are close to writing exams. I am planning to delay telling them as long as I can. Maybe I will wait until they confront me, because I can't face doing it."

One day at a time, they finally agreed. Then they ate their lunch in silence.

As 1990 ended and the clock struck midnight, fireworks lit up the sky. From the townships to the villages, screams of jubilation rang out and prayers were sent up to God. What was uppermost in the minds of many was the promise of a new year.

Along Durban's Golden Mile beachfront, beer was flowing and the revelers floated in the smoky cloud of roasting meat, intoxicated by anticipation of better things to come.

Even the stingiest were encouraged to spend freely; to the delight of the children, sweets and cakes were in abundance.

In the midst of all this, nauseated Zola was gripped by fear and guilt. She felt alone. She locked herself in the tiny toilet at home, puked her guts out, and cried rivers. At sixteen, she had lost her innocence. "Your father will kill you before he allows you to give birth at such a young age," a voice inside taunted her.

Her father's temper was legendary. It was not for nothing that he was known as "Pure Chilli," the hottest spice in Durban, that land of assfire curries.

In this solo misery, Zola entered the New Year, while keeping up appearances in front of her parents. Even when she tried to forget, the pit in her growing stomach made her sick with worry. She began wearing oversized jackets, T-shirts, and elastic-waisted bottoms. They did not raise an alarm as both her parents encouraged her to hide her body from prying predators.

Her body grew, filling in to cushion the life growing inside her. MaSosibo fought her female intuition. She tried to allow herself to believe that her daughter's body was simply changing from a girl's into a young woman's. But lying to yourself has a way of making you sick. MaSosibo woke up night after night in a cold sweat. She lost sleep as she agonized over what she knew, but did not want to acknowledge.

CHAPTER SIX

Life in Durban's Mkhumbane township was buzzing with new hope, and the *shebeens* were making more money than ever. Patrons were in jovial moods with the promise of imminent riches. Those with lively imaginations spoke of living in mansions with servants, fleets of cars, and travels to countries they had only heard of.

A fermented pineapple drink, and *isqatha*, the lethal homebrew that sometimes included battery acid, fueled dreams of an imminent new land of milk and honey. Under a cloud of intoxicating marijuana, patrons sat from mid-morning till dusk, drinking and dreaming of a life where their wealthier selves would be realized.

Skwiza, Zola's aunt the *shebeen* queen with a string of taverns across Mkhumbane, looked on with satisfaction as her patrons used their meager salaries, earned from tending suburban gardens, to drink and fuel their dreams. Like many of the women in her family, she was tall. In addition, she had large breasts that burdened her with back problems, forcing her to lean forward when she walked. This leaning accentuated her large behind and pushed it even further out. Her knock-kneed twigs for legs carried the heavy load that was her two-meter self. Her stature was both comical and fearsome. She was very warm at the sight of money, and terrifyingly icy when her patrons couldn't pay their debts.

She was the opposite of Zola's mother, who was matronly towards her children and a submissive servant to her dominating husband. Zola loved her aunt and was in awe wherever they had the rare opportunity of visiting her.

The feeling was mutual. Skwiza loved Zola because she was beautiful and young, and reminded her of herself when she was Zola's age. Young people kept Skwiza alive.

It was obvious to Zola that once her secret was uncovered, that was where she would go for shelter. Skwiza was the only woman who stood up to her father. In fact, she towered over him in her stilettos. Pure Chilli did not like Skwiza for this reason. It was clear to Zola that something about her unsettled him, and he did not want his family near this woman.

When school opened, Zola had three months to go. Her muscles were no longer pronounced and toned. She was rounder, but youth with its inexperienced eyes did not suspect anything. Pearl and Mr. Zondo, however, knew what was going on underneath the uniform. She no longer took part in practice, but sat on the side and watched. It drove the coach mad, but she chalked Zola's reluctance up to the fickleness of teenagers. "She had been slowing down anyway. A new Zola Budd will emerge from the new batch. You watch and see." The coach was ever the optimist.

Sporo was distracted from his game since the new term began. He could not stop worrying about the secret he and Zola were keeping. He wanted to tell his parents, but he knew that they would immediately show up on Zola's doorstep to report the matter. So he became her accomplice.

Deep in thought about Zola, he did not see the speeding taxi as he and the team crossed the road from practice. The screams were too late and all went blank. Sporo and two other teammates were cut down by the runaway taxi. Zola with a baby in her arms was the last image he saw before he surrendered.

His muscles softened. The bloodied ball rolled away from

him. The coach crouched and called, "Sporo, Sporo!" His eyes were open but not registering the coach, who was frantic, crying, swearing, and cradling Sporo's head. Some boys ran towards the school to tell the principal, and others began to stone the taxi. The driver was dazed. He had been rushing to pick up an extra load of people who would pay him and not the owner of the taxi.

When Zola saw the bloodied boys crying openly, coming towards her class, water began to leave her body, coursing down her thighs. At first, when she felt this warmth coming out of her, she thought she was peeing, but the water kept coming. She stood up, her eyes wide with shock. Teacher Pearl took one look at her and knew she could not wait. Pearl met the boys at the door as she shouted for Mr. Zondo to help drive Zola to hospital. The nearest was Marianhill.

The boys blurted out the shocking news of the accident and pandemonium followed. Mr. Zondo took the wheel and stepped on the petrol as Pearl held Zola on the back seat. They were forced to stop and deliver the baby in the car because Zola could not wait. She had heard what the boys had said and her body wanted the baby out.

He was gone. Her life support was gone. Now it was just her and this baby.

Pearl and Mr. Zondo decided to take the young mother and baby to the Pinetown Clinic. When they got there, they were sent to the maternity ward of the King Edward Hospital. She had bled badly.

The news that Zola had given birth came as no surprise to maSosibo. She was relieved, and secretly excited. Of course she pretended to be just as surprised as her husband was when he turned to stone. All he said was, "I have no daughter. She and her bastard are not welcome in this house. She has brought us nothing but shame."

His words left maSosibo with no strength to argue. The next day she sneaked out to go and see Zola at the hospital while her husband was at work. Zola was grieving the death of Sporo and preoccupied with the baby. Like her father, she had turned to stone. She was silent while a million thoughts were racing through her mind about her next plan.

The sight of her mother did not frighten her. She simply showed her the baby but did not speak, except to say that she would move in with her Aunt Skwiza in Mkhumbane. Her mother protested mildly, but she knew it was the only option.

Zola apologized to her mother for shaming her, and asked her please to relay the message to her father. They held each other and cried, before maSosibo kissed her new granddaughter and left.

Zola remembered that Sporo had said if the baby was a girl, she should be named Nomvelo, "as beautiful as you." His words came back to haunt her. When Zola went to register the baby, she wrote down her name as Nomvelo Zulu, and the address of Skwiza's *shebeen*.

On discharge day, she rolled the baby into the blanket that her mother had given her and headed to Mkhumbane for a new life in the *shebeen* with Aunt Skwiza, who welcomed Zola and Mvelo with open arms.

Nothing was for free with Skwiza. Zola had to work for her keep. She helped with fermenting the pineapple and bread for the homebrewed alcohol, she cleaned the house, and did whatever else Skwiza asked her to do. But as much as she worked Zola, Skwiza made sure that she and the baby were taken good care of. Secretly, Skwiza was grateful to have the chance of living with real family, with blood ties.

In Mkhumbane, Zola closed the chapter on her youth. She did not attend Sporo's funeral.

Occasionally she heard from her mother, who had been forbidden to keep in contact with her. Zola didn't attempt to go back to school or contact Sporo's family. She simply concentrated on her baby and working in the *shebeen*.

She was not one to pay any attention to men. Sporo had been special. The men in the *shebeen* did not interest her. Their addiction to alcohol seemed weak to her. She watched them from a distance and they seemed to sense that she was not someone to try their luck with. She was cold and indifferent to their antics.

Mvelo grew in the midst of the chaos of the *shebeen*. She was four years old when people headed for the ballot box to vote for the first time. There was a lot of jubilation and music all around her. She clapped her little hands and danced along with everyone.

She was a delightful toddler who was spoiled by Skwiza and the patrons, who offered her treats to get Zola's affections. Mvelo simply called her "Skwiza," like everybody else, when really she should have been calling her Gogo. But Skwiza would have been mortified. Aging was something that repulsed her. "It smells of death," she said. So everyone just called her Skwiza.

In the middle of all this jubilation, one day the phone rang and Skwiza fell on her knees, crying out to God. Zola's parents were dead. Her father was accused of supporting the wrong political party and a vigilante youth group poured petrol in their house and set it alight with them inside. "My sister is gone, Zola, she's gone. Oh God." Skwiza folded herself into the fetal position and howled. She frightened little Mvelo who had never seen her like this.

Zola remained dry-eyed and went numb inside. The church dominated the funeral and the burial. They did not acknowledge Zola and the baby in case she got any ideas about claiming an inheritance. Her father had bequeathed his pension and savings that should have been for her higher education to the church as sole beneficiary. She did not contest it and discouraged Skwiza from doing so as well. The turn of events brought Skwiza and Zola closer than before. Zola and Mvelo were the only two remaining blood relatives that Skwiza knew of.

Business was booming at Skwiza's *shebeen*. While the black middle-class emerged and headed for the suburbs, on weekends they sojourned at Skwiza's for beers, meat, and township flavor.

In this exodus from townships to suburbs, a lawyer called Sipho Mdletshe stayed put. He was Skwiza's favorite customer because he not only bought his own drinks but he also bought rounds for others who clung to him like bees to honey.

Skwiza was proud of him because he was acquainted with highly respected leaders in society, but his friends were the customers at her Mkhumbane *shebeen*. This was a calculated self-protective measure on his part. He became close to those who were socially beneath him because they couldn't hurt him. Instead they looked up to him.

While his colleagues headed towards upmarket Mount Edgecombe and Umhlanga in their fancy Hummers and Z3s, he would go in his humble yellow Getz from his fancy office with its view of the Durban harbor to his modest house in Mkhumbane.

His colleagues referred to his township as Cato Manor, but he reminded them that George Christopher Cato was some bugger born in England, probably a misfit in his own country, who then came to take his chances in the land of the naïve natives. They were so gullible that they allowed some of their land to be named after him, calling it his manor. "The audacity of these colonists is mind-boggling," Sipho would say, stating that he was perfectly happy with Mkhumbane, a vibrant old community named after a little stream that ran through the historic township, and making it clear that the subject was now closed.

He would go to the *shebeen* every evening with *umngenandlini*, presents for little Mvelo and for Zola. Mostly chocolates for Mvelo, which he sometimes gave her secretly because Zola did not approve of too many sweets, and Zola got fruit and biscuits called Oreos. His gifts did come with expectations of affection from Zola, and Mvelo latched on to him. She called him *babayi*, claiming him as her dad.

He had an easy manner that reminded Zola of Sporo but she fought these feelings as best as she could. He was a known ladies man, a womanizer, and he didn't hide the fact. He was tall, but he loved all kinds of women, tall and short, fat and thin, young and old, black and white, they came to him in their numbers. This made it easy for Zola to dismiss him, because she was not interested in sharing him.

Sipho was trying to use a nonchalant exterior to hook Zola, but he was beginning to think it wouldn't work. This was new to him, feeling so helpless with the rock that this woman seemed to be. He had tried to persuade her with gifts, by loving her daughter, and even ignoring her. But none of it seemed to work.

At first he felt very sad for her because she looked haunted by something that had hurt her so badly that she had stopped living. He watched her working at Skwiza's, clearing tables in her distant way, as if she were alone in the middle of the rowdy crowd. He noticed her toned muscles from lifting the beer crates.

"Forget about it, my bra, this one is for the angels," said his drunkard of a brother. "She must have been hurt real bad.

She is out of circulation, not for sale, unlike your gold diggers who are with you for your money."

Sipho laughed at him and said everybody wanted to be loved.

"Oh, rest assured, she will be loved." He paused meaningfully. "By me," he announced. And they both laughed raucously and continued to drink.

On the stroke of midnight, when 1994 closed with renewed hope, Zola drank a bottle of cider and felt light in the head. She was swept up in the spirit of celebrating the new democracy and wanted to close the chapter that had been so painful for her. The new year held promise, as she watched her four-year-old daughter grow to be a sassy little princess with the easy attitude of her late father. Zola felt proud that she had at least accomplished this in her twenty years of life.

In her tipsy state, she laughed and danced around with Mvelo. Sipho could not believe his eyes. He knew that if ever there was a chance for him, it was now. He cut in and offered his hand to Zola, pleading with his eyes. Mvelo gave her mother a shove that made her fall forward into Sipho's arms. The music slowed and Sipho took his cue. His drunken brother looked on with his mouth hanging open in disbelief and envy.

And in that moment, those four years of flirting culminated into a relationship between Sipho and Zola. But it was with a strict condition from Zola. "I will not share you with anyone. If that is a problem for you, speak now and let's go our separate ways."

Sipho was silent. He was so enjoying the moment that he did not want to deal with this "all or nothing" stand. A few tense, silent moments passed before he responded. "All I know for sure is that I don't want to lose you. I will do my best to be faithful to you, but if I am unable to keep my promise, I will be honest with you." As he said these words, he felt something tighten around his neck.

When he told his friends about how this girl was different from any other girl he'd dated, how he was both miserable and indescribably happy, how he couldn't stop thinking about her and her sweet little daughter, they all said the same thing: "Perhaps for the first time in your thirty-six years, you are in love." Then he felt even more panic-stricken. He was distracted and couldn't work or concentrate for long without recalling Zola's dry and clever jokes.

One day he went to the *shebeen* and asked Skwiza for her blessing to have Zola and Mvelo move in with him. She gave him a hug and laughed. To her, Zola couldn't have chosen a better man. Besides the obvious benefit of having Sipho the lawyer as her son-in-law if it led to marriage, she really wanted Zola to find happiness. Love had already transformed her into a quietly blossoming flower. Sipho had brought a small, happy song to Zola's lips. Anyone with an ear for music could hear there was talent lying dormant in her. Until now, Mvelo was the only one who had cracked her open with a love that couldn't remain indifferent.

When Sipho proposed to Zola that she and Mvelo should come home, Zola looked confused. "But we are home," she said.

"No, I mean you should come home with me. You and Mvelo belong with me. Please say you will move in with me."

She was resistant. "I don't think that Aunt Skwiza would—"

"I have already asked her blessing," he assured Zola, "and she said yes. Please say yes, you belong with me."

And so Zola agreed, but first she had to speak to Mvelo.

Again Sipho was one step ahead of her. He had asked what the little princess thought of the arrangement, and she had answered him by jumping up and down.

So they moved into his house not far from the *shebeen*, and those were good times for Zola. Remembering what it was like to have a family, she threw herself into creating a home for Mvelo and Sipho.

It was a long time before Sipho plucked up the courage to take her to visit his overbearing and possessive mother in the rural area of eMpendle. At the back of his mind, he knew it was a bad idea, but Zola wanted it and he wanted to make her happy. Since the loss of her own family, she had begun to crave a sense of belonging. She missed her mother and thought perhaps Sipho's mother could fill that void in time. "Am I not good enough to meet your family?" she had asked him when Sipho once more evaded the issue. He finally gave in, and they packed their bags for the weekend and headed to the homestead.

At the sight of Mvelo, who he explained was Zola's child, it was over before it started. Sipho's mother looked straight through Zola, and resisted the charms of little Mvelo. She called her son aside and gave him a tongue-lashing. "How long are you going to keep bringing these unsuitable girls into your father's house? This girl has no meat on her bones. Look at her, she is all muscles like a man. Her behind is an ironing board. Not to mention her having a child with some other man. She is second-hand, Sipho, *iskeni*. You are better than that."

Sipho steeled himself and took it, not knowing that Zola had overheard.

Zola repacked the bags and asked to be driven back immediately. "I heard everything, Sipho. I am sorry that I insisted to come. I was wrong. I will spare her the pain of pretending." She was surprised by how much it hurt to be rejected by this woman whom she had never met. The next time she would see Sipho's mother would be years later, under very different circumstances.

The drive home was very subdued. Tears were dangerously close to spilling down Zola's cheeks. Sipho drove with one hand and held her hand with the other.

Mvelo sat very quietly at the back. She knew something was wrong.

Just as what begins as a small pimple can end up as a festering sore, cracks began to show in their happy home. Sipho began to work long hours, sneaking back home in the middle of the night. When he was there, dinners were tense and no longer filled with laughter and stories from the day at the office. Like a turtle, Zola retreated back into her shell and became her old sad self again.

Mvelo tried hard to keep her family entertained, but it didn't work. The house was cold and she became angry, mostly at her mother. "Why can't she just be happy?" she would ask herself.

Zola's sadness was infectious. It seeped into everything and repelled Sipho to stay at the office or the *shebeen*.

Zola sensed she was losing him. She felt angry at him for not standing up for her with his mother and at herself for failing to keep him interested in her. A wave of panic came over her each time she thought of the future without Sipho. She fought hard to fight back the tears when she looked at Mvelo. What would become of this child? She knew she could not stay with Sipho if he began sleeping around with other women. The talk of the deadly HIV-AIDS sent shivers down her spine. She swore to herself that she would not contract the disease and leave Mvelo alone.

But she was her own worst enemy and, hard as Sipho tried to keep the family together, she pushed him further away. She worried and panicked that he was not being honest with her and she would contract the disease, so she rejected his

advances. She demanded tests and insisted on condoms.
Rules tightened the noose around Sipho's neck, until one day
he woke up choking and could no longer remember why he
was with this woman. He didn't know how to tell her, and his
bond with Mvelo made it harder.

CHAPTER SEVEN

Sipho loved Zola. He had been with her alone for six whole years. But it had got too tricky for him. Women loved him and he loved women. "It is just unnatural for me," he told Zola.

She tried to turn a blind eye until he came home one day with a party of visiting American lawyers from work. Among them was a woman who was very beautiful. They had dinner at Sipho's house and then they went off to the *shebeen*, for a "township experience." At dinner it was clear to Zola that his charm had won her over.

Unlike most African-Americans, Nonceba Hlathi was umXhosa who went to live in the States with her African-American grandmother, Mae. Her name came as a surprise to the locals. She looked so exotic, they expected her to have an English name. But she was forceful about her heritage and identity. She made it known by constantly engaging Sipho in her mother tongue. The Americans were fascinated and broke into fits of giggles at the click sounds. She and Sipho enjoyed showing off the language to the other guests.

Nonceba's skin had a golden tone and glowed as if the sun was shining on her. Her cheekbones were chiseled, and she had sharp eyes that did not miss anything. She wore her hair in braids. Sipho was as charmed by her as she was by him. Their shameless banter made the others look at each other with surprise. They had never seen Nonceba flirting. They called her the ice queen behind her back. Seeing her softening like this amazed them, and Sipho intrigued them because of it.

But Nonceba was unaware of the misery she was causing Zola. Sipho had not been honest about the nature of his relationship with Zola. He remained vague, saying she was a close friend in need and that he was looking after her and her daughter. The way he said it, it sounded to Nonceba as if Zola was a live-in helper whom he was assisting to get back on her feet. It didn't help that Zola remained distant and cold towards Sipho in their presence. She retreated to her room and ate her dinner alone while the lively conversation went on at the dinner table.

Zola was a natural beauty, but contrasted against this woman, she did not see the light of day. She knew it and, after serving dinner and holding pretentious small talk, fearful Zola excused herself and went to bed.

She could hear the sounds of laughter and intelligent conversation going on, until Sipho moved the party to Skwiza's. Skwiza was thrilled to have visitors from America.

This was the loneliest night for Zola since she had come to live with Sipho, because she knew it was the anticipated end of the dream, and she cried herself to sleep. Mvelo couldn't sleep either, but for a different reason. She couldn't stop thinking of the beautiful woman from America, and she vowed that one day she would be as beautiful as her.

At ten years old, Mvelo had little understanding about matters of the heart. While her mother was devastated, she wasn't, because she knew without a doubt that Sipho loved them.

The millennium was looming with a new chapter for Zola. When they broke up, Sipho had sat both Zola and Mvelo down. It was a solemn and tense moment. He was emotional. He apologized for failing to keep his promise. And then he openly declared a different kind of love he now felt for Nonceba. He stressed that nothing would stop him from being a father to

Mvelo, and how much he still loved them both, but Nonceba was somebody that he did not want to lose.

Mvelo's eyes were big with tears. She looked from her mother to Sipho with confusion. She couldn't believe that he was ripping their hearts apart. She loved Sipho, but her mother was her world. She ran out of the room and locked herself in her bedroom. Sipho felt defeated. It was hard watching his little girl hurt because of him, but he wanted to speak grown-up talk with Zola.

He had thought about his speech for days, but it was hard to find the words. He had begun to realize what was happening to him. The love he felt for Zola was the safe kind that most men want. They choose a woman who is not challenging to them so they can have a comfortable and predictable life. They choose someone who will cook and take care of their home and meet their physical needs, who they can provide for, and who will simply admire and love them in return.

Nonceba on the other hand had been like a bolt of lightning. With Zola, he was balanced because he had control, but with Nonceba he was treading on more dangerous ground. He said it was out of respect for Zola that he did not want to lie to her.

He didn't seem to consider that Zola might pack up her things and leave. In his love fever for Nonceba, he simply assumed that Zola would accept it and continue to stay with him. He knew she had nowhere to go but back to the *shebeen*. And he knew she didn't want the growing Mvelo to be exposed to lecherous, drunk men.

Zola may not have been in the same league as Nonceba, but she was a woman with her own pride and she loved Sipho too much to share him. She didn't waste any time before she packed up hers and Mvelo's clothing. As a parting shot, she poured a bucket of water over his bed and peed on his shoes, and they headed back to where they had started with Skwiza, who welcomed them again with open arms and cooed over them. She was also unhappy with Nonceba, this new woman in Sipho's life, because he was no longer a regular customer.

Nonceba was a complex woman. She was descended from those who had died with blood-curdling screams and curses on their tongues; and those who were in touch with the earth in ways that empirical science could not explain. Her name meant "mother of sympathy," and she was born in a small holding cell at John Vorster Square. Her mother, Zimkitha Hlathi, was in jail, but she was a free and defiant spirit. On the other hand, her father, Johan Steyn, was racked with worry for Zimkitha, his forbidden love.

Now Nonceba's feminine curves echoed the strong and proud Ashanti queen Yaa Asantewa, Sojourner Truth, Nongqawuze, Ellen Khuzwayo, Lillian Ngoyi and many warrior women of the world. Her will was fierce and resolute, like the defiant Boeremeisies who resisted English rule. She had the restlessness of Ingrid Jonker and the makings of a powerful *sangoma* in her but she did not want to acknowledge it.

She had the kind of hair that many black women spend thousands of rands to achieve, yet she longed for cotton candy kinky hair, a broad nose, and the fuller curves that were associated with authentic blackness. While many black women envied her, she envied them.

She hated the attention that she got because she did not trust it. She knew it was mostly based on her looks. But she had other gifts. She was intuitive about those who crossed her path. As a child, it made her sick because the heavy weight of all the sadness and sickness in the world was too much for a child to bear. The American doctors diagnosed her with all kinds of names and gave her pills, but over time she learned to manage her sensitivity.

Meeting Sipho calmed her down because she trusted that his love was for the real her, and not simply for the outside package. She could finally breathe out. She made a good lawyer because she could detach from the argument, but instinctively gauge the weaker side and then go in for the kill.

Sipho became a changed man in ways that frustrated many people in Mkhumbane because he was no longer available to them as he had been. The *tsostis* who used to rely on his representation in court, for crimes big and small, could no longer call on him because he began engaging in bigger corporate representation, at Nonceba's suggestion. They thought of ambushing her, but they sensed that she was not alone. They felt she had other souls hovering about her, so each time they came close, they would feel shivers down their spines.

The person who was most unimpressed with Nonceba was Sipho's mother. "I don't like her one bit," she said, when he took Nonceba to visit the old woman in eMpendle. "She scares me. There is something not right with that girl. She has the ancient ones, *amadlozi*, all over her. What is wrong with a good Zulu woman like Zola?"

Sipho nearly fell over when he remembered the disparaging things she had said about Zola. "Well, better the devil we know," she muttered, when she saw the look he gave her, "than this strangeness you are now bringing to my home."

Sipho never took Nonceba back to the village after that, and it was on one of his weekend visits to eMpendle that the *tsotsis* took their chance. They saw his car was gone and thought they would wait until the middle of the night so they could ambush Nonceba in a confused state of sleep. They had learned this trick from the Boers back in the eighties when they raided the townships in the stillness of the night. The *tsotsis* aimed for the early hours of Sunday when only the spirits of the dead dared to roam the streets.

The house was perfectly dark as they got closer. They knew everything about the house because when Skwiza kicked them out to close the *shebeen*, the party had often moved to Sipho's house. That was before the arrival of this curse, Nonceba.

They reckoned it would be easy. Sipho had no burglar bars. He lived as if he was removed from the world around him. He always said that living behind high fences and alarms simply enriched the security businesses that preyed on people's fear. The *tsotsis* thought this was a good philosophy to have.

The last one of the four *tsotsis* had just managed to climb into the dining room when the window snapped shut behind them. They looked at each other in silence, their eyes bulging. The house was sweating like a sauna and there was a strong smell of herbs. They stood there, transfixed, not knowing what their next move should be. Then Nonceba came out of the bedroom, carrying a clay pot. She sprinkled the contents of the pot around the house. She didn't seem to see them standing there. She was talking to herself in a language they could not comprehend. The sound of it brought goosebumps to their skin.

She went into the bathroom, and the dogs began to howl, which jolted them into action. One climbed on a chair trying to open the window, but it wouldn't budge, so they headed for the door and tumbled out, too shocked to utter a sound.

No one ever knew what changed these four from thugs to tea-drinking churchgoers. Not even among themselves did they care to talk about that night when they tried to attack Nonceba.

◆───◇───◆

CHAPTER EIGHT

Zola's stay with Skwiza wasn't long. She worked fast with some of Skwiza's patrons who had found space and material to build a shack for her in a mushrooming squatter camp on the margins of Mkhumbane. She was hurt, and afraid for her daughter. Stories of child rape spurred her on to work fast to get Mvelo out of the *shebeen* and harm's way. Zola was quiet by nature, but now, in her private pain, her silence was loaded with fear and rage and disappointment. It was so deep that she couldn't bring herself to feel it. She just focused on survival and making a home for Mvelo. She began to look for work and sold second-hand clothes in town.

It was hard for them, especially when it rained. Water would come through the cracks in the walls. Nature was cruel. It felt as if God was spitting on them. During horrible, windy storms, they held their hearts, praying that their shack wouldn't get blown away. The wind was a bully, shoving them around.

Then there were the smells. A nasty combination of rotting food and stale urine. They had a neighbor with irritable bowels and could hear every labored sound as he conducted his business in the bucket. They only had six long drop toilets in the area, so people improvised with buckets, especially at night.

Some nights there would be sounds that made Zola very uncomfortable. She was especially unhappy about Mvelo hearing them, and would turn the radio up to drown out the moans next door. She never did explain why their neighbors sometimes made these noises at night. Ever perceptive, Mvelo didn't push the issue because she knew even before asking that she shouldn't.

Their first winter in the shacks was terrible. They survived three runaway fires that were triggered by neighbors' paraffin stoves falling over. Zola and Mvelo were saved by having their shack right next to the road. Those in the middle always had to start over, with nothing but the corrugated iron saved from the fire.

In one of those fires, a young boy died. He was asleep when it started. By the time his mother ran from the *shebeen* to their shack, it was too late.

It was clear from that woman's gut wrenching screams of agony that somebody somewhere would have bad luck for life. They had to pin her down to stop her from lunging into the flames. It was a pathetic sight, her dress flying up and her bloomers with big holes on display, as she fought off those who were stopping her from getting to her son.

Newshounds were right on cue with cameras, notepads, and the same tired questions for the mother in pain. "How do you feel about your son dying in a burning shack?"

"My son just burned into charcoal, how the fuck do you think I am feeling?" the grieving woman screamed, hailing insults at the cowering journalists.

The next day, newspaper headlines were asking who was responsible for this structural violence. Zola gave Mvelo many lectures about the dangers of playing with matchboxes and anything that could start a fire.

Sipho lay low for a while, waiting for Zola to calm down, and then he came to see them. He offered to help with Mvelo's schooling and things for the house. What he felt for Zola was beyond what a lover felt. He had some form of familial responsibility.

His offer brought out all of Zola's pent up scorn and anger. She kept shouting at him, "We have known each other half my life, all the years you claimed to love me, and when I finally gave in and opened my heart to you, Sipho, what do you do? You thank me with a plate of shit." Her voice was bitter with anger and fear and confusion about why Sipho now loved somebody else.

She was trying to hit him with pots and hurling plates at him. He ducked, and went towards her, taking her blows until she fell against his chest exhausted, and cried like a small child. He rocked her to sleep, and then the three of them slept until he woke up in the middle of the night.

He covered mother and child with a blanket and left a wad of R200 notes to rid himself of guilt, convincing himself that he was still a good guy. Then he walked out into a silver night lightened by the moon.

Once, he had told little Mvelo to look at the moon and asked her to tell him what she saw inside it. They were lying on their backs on his lawn. "It looks like there is someone living inside it," she had said, sitting up and looking into his eyes for confirmation.

"Hmm, yes, I think so. It looks like a woman carrying a baby on her back and firewood on her head," he said, outlining a picture with his finger. He said it so convincingly little Mvelo actually saw it as he explained.

"Yes, I can see it too," she said, jumping up and down with excitement and making herself giddy.

He broke into his laugh and they collapsed into a laughing bundle. Zola stood there, quietly amused but trying to be stern, rebuking them for making noise at night like village witches. He thought nostalgically about that time as he headed back to his home that he now shared with Nonceba.

After some months had passed, Zola could tell that Mvelo really missed Sipho and wanted to see him. She softened because she couldn't stand seeing her daughter pining, and allowed her to visit Sipho and Nonceba at the house.

This became a highlight for Mvelo, who had moved on from the anger of the break up with her mother and returned to loving the only father figure she had ever known. It was awkward at first, because she was openly resentful of Nonceba. Secretly, she thought Nonceba was the most beautiful woman she had ever seen and wanted to be friends with her, but her loyalty was with her rejected mother. She acted up to make Sipho's woman suffer, but it wasn't working. Instead Nonceba disarmed her with her charm and seemed to know exactly what her favorite things were. It wasn't long before they were firm friends. But she kept up pretenses with her mother. With Zola, she acted like she wasn't overly impressed with Nonceba.

Mvelo had adjusted to living in the shacks. She played with children there, but she didn't like it when kids from brick houses looked down on her at school. She learned quickly that children can be mean. She also learned to reject them before they rejected her. The kids in the shacks would stick together, giving her comfort and even confidence.

A researcher from England came to do a study on the shacks and was surprised to discover the confidence levels of children there were higher than many of those living in proper houses. The children liked him because he gave them sweets and cakes, but Nonceba spoiled it for them when she chased him away.

She had seen him several times when she came to pick Mvelo up. She asked Mvelo about him and Mvelo told her about his questions and how they enjoyed his sweets. "He speaks like the people on TV," Mvelo told Nonceba.

When the researcher's study began to make the rounds in the papers and on radio stations, Nonceba thought it was time. His conclusions seemed to suggest that the shacks were not so bad; the children were happy and coping with the situation. Never mind the casualties of fire from paraffin stoves because there was no electricity. No mention of the lack of space or privacy that exposed young children to adult sexual activities.

Nonceba pounced on the researcher the next time she saw him. "Are there no children in England? Why would you fly all the way from there to do your study here?" He tried to reason with her but he was no match for her. "You can't fool me. You can't fool them either." She pointed at the children. "It's your sweets that they like, not your study, and they've read you well. They shape their answers to suit what they know you want to hear."

She hit the home truths and drew blood with her sharp words. Then she calmly watched him slink into his car, red-faced and furious, on his way to find some other shantytown on the continent, still avoiding the problems in his own country.

Mvelo was shocked and embarrassed because Nonceba was right. They did answer in ways that made the researcher happy because they wanted to get the sweets. In the shacks, children liked to imagine happy houses with all the trappings. They took comfort in dreaming because all things are possible there. If their teachers asked them to write an essay entitled "My Home," in these compositions they all lived in mansions with stables of horses to ride around green hills; their fathers, although in real life most of them didn't know their fathers, were owners of chocolate factories where they ate chocolate until they were sick; and their mothers, most of whom were domestic workers, were pretty and wore expensive clothes and perfumes. The children were mostly imagining their female teachers.

Mvelo learnt many things from Nonceba. Nonceba loved head-wraps and colorful African prints. She never shopped from chain stores. Everything she wore made her look pretty. In her early teens, Mvelo was insecure inside, but she portrayed a different exterior. She began to mimic Nonceba's style, in the hope that she too would be pretty like her. Her friends laughed at her and her African print dresses, but she didn't mind because Nonceba said it was OK to be different. It hurt at first when others laughed but she began to truly believe in being OK with the way she was.

At first it was Nonceba's words that kept her strong, but soon it was her own inner voice growing confident. She began to look at herself in the mirror and realize that she could never look like Nonceba. She was darker, her hair was kinkier, and her nose was broader. Her hips and behind were also filling out. But the way she looked no longer repulsed her as it had at first. It made her curious and excited.

Nonceba chose to speak her mother tongue. She responded in isiXhosa to her other black colleagues at the law firm, who preferred to speak English, even among themselves.

IsiXhosa was her language. She and her grandmother had used it between themselves when they moved back to the States. It was the only thing her grandmother Mae could hold on to after she gave in and decided to go back to the country of her birth. They did not want to forget that they were Africans. Mae had ditched her surname, Wilson, and proudly declared herself Mrs. Mae Hlathi when she had married the good doctor, Nonceba's grandfather.

Sometimes Sipho felt sorry for the interns at the office. They would come in bright-eyed, willing to do anything to have Nonceba as a mentor because she was a light-skinned American. CJay, whose real name was Cetshwayo Jama Zulu, received Nonceba's standard response. He came in with a pseudo-American accent, thinking that he would schmooze Nonceba with his charms, which never failed him on campus.

"Right, let's begin with getting to know you. What is your full name?" Nonceba asked, looking at his CV.

"My name is CJay," said Cetshwayo.

"I see that," she said, "but who are your people, CJay?"

He looked confused.

"I mean, if I stripped away your cool act, who will I meet?"

Now CJay was getting pissed off. "Yo, man, look, cut a brotha some slack. I'm just lookin' to finish my credits and get myself a job to make some dough. Know what I'm sayin'?"

"CJay, have you lived in America?" Nonceba was keen to cut through the bullshit.

His eyes shone. There was no better compliment for him than this, an American thinking he was the real thing. "Oh no, doll, it's just something I picked up." He grinned like the fool he was.

"Firstly," Nonceba was done with having her time wasted, "I am not your doll. And secondly, you don't fool anyone except yourself with this nonsense, Cetshwayo Jama Ka Zulu. Listen to the sound of it. The southern Nguni language is a beautiful thing. Why do you want to pretend to be a half-baked American? You come from a long line of proud people, but instead you've chosen a path of faking accents and a rootless existence. You use this language with bitch this and bitch that. You think it is so cool to go around calling yourselves nigga this and nigga that. Do you even know the pain that is pulsating in this hybrid of a language that you have taken and claimed as your own?

"Cetshwayo, you don't know how lucky you are. Child, you

make me want to weep for your proud ancestors. Through your name, you can trace yourself back to Shaka, that beautiful son of a defiant mother Nandi, his aunt Mkabayi who strategically ruled the Zulu kingdom from behind the scenes, and even further back to his grandfather Jama ka Ndaba.

"Leave things that you don't know about to television. I can see that you're intelligent, your transcript shows that. And I want to give you a chance. So I'd like you to come and intern for us." And just like that she smiled and extended her hand to Cetshwayo, who was now totally mute, as if his tongue had been cut out of him.

CHAPTER NINE

Gradually, Zola swallowed her pride and allowed Sipho to assist with Mvelo's school fees and pocket money. But when he said that he wanted to send Mvelo to a school in town, she flatly refused. For once she and Nonceba were in agreement. Although Zola's reasoning was different from Nonceba's. She was concerned about her daughter's living arrangements, that she would be teased by children with rich parents because she lived in eMkhukhwini, the shacks, while they lived in posh places.

Nonceba was surprised that Sipho would want Mvelo to go into a system that would steadily poison her. "She will get a better education there, please let's not argue on this one, Nonceba," he sighed.

"But Sipho, you know what happens at those schools. The girls take purgative pills to flatten their stomachs like ballerinas. She will unlearn all that she has learned about herself so far. She will want to slice her nose thinner and break her back just to be noticed." She reminded Sipho about his niece Nomusa, from the *bundus* of eMpendle, who had tried to commit suicide after he had enrolled her in a private boarding school and she found she no longer fitted in anywhere.

Suicide always touched a nerve with Nonceba. Her mother had walked into the ocean. She was just a year old but she knew the horror and the shock of it.

Sipho tried to reason with Nonceba, saying that Mvelo

was stronger and different from Nomusa. But she wasn't convinced. "What is wrong with the schools here where her friends are?" she challenged Sipho.

He said township schools were ill-equipped, that the teachers were not well-trained, and the children were misbehaving.

"And they don't misbehave in the private schools? Do you see girls in the township schools puking and shitting their guts out because they want to be thin?"

"No, but I see them pregnant, Nonceba. Not just one or two, but quite a few of them," Sipho shot back.

"Girls in private schools get pregnant too; they just pop in to the Marie Stopes Clinic and have an abortion."

"So what are you saying, Nonceba, that it is better to populate the township than going to Marie Stopes?" He was exasperated. Her arguments were always out of step with everyone else.

"I am saying, why do you have so much faith in the private and Model C schools? Black middle-class parents like you should put their energies into the public schools, your own old schools here at home, not in town. I mean, why pay thousands of rands for fees, transport, endless field trips and even salaries for private tutors when you can fix a school here and let the children learn for twelve years, having paid less than two thousand rands per year? Hell, university fees are nothing compared to what is forked out for these private schools. Can't you see the message? They are trying to keep out the riff-raff by putting up the fees. And a child will not develop neuroses about her blackness in a local school.

"All these educated people shouldn't be putting their faith in private schools just because they're fancy and they're in town. Their resources should be invested here. We won't have a class issue then, this new racism where certain blacks are called Boss and Madam. The apartheid that the masses fought against, we are now doing it to ourselves. What I am saying is that I want to protect Mvelo. I want her whole. If she needs to learn English, I will teach her in addition to what she is learning in the township school. And I will teach her the kind of history that she needs to learn, not the version that they will teach her about Shaka being a ruthless cannibal. I will give her the gifts that I was lucky to receive from my grandmother that are not in the pages of any history book."

She put her arms seductively around Sipho and he melted. He agreed to everything that she asked of him. First order of the day for Nonceba, with Zola's permission of course, was to accompany Mvelo to school. She wanted to meet her teachers and introduce herself. After Nonceba shook hands with all of them, Mvelo knew that she had noticed something about Mr. Zwide, the History teacher. Nonceba had asked to speak to him in private. After collecting his tongue that was practically hanging out, he must have foolishly thought Nonceba was flirting with him.

He was mistaken. What Nonceba wanted to do was to warn him. "Listen to me very carefully, Mr. Zwide. I see you. I can see that you are abusing your power and taking advantage of these teenage girls. Just know that if you ever so much as look at Mvelo the wrong way, I will be onto you like a ton of bricks."

Between Zola, Sipho and Nonceba, Mvelo was in a good place.

When Nomagugu, a drama student at the University of Natal, came with the gospel of reviving traditions like virginity testing, Zola said Mvelo should go. She said it was a good measure to protect her from boys and lurking perverts. To make Zola happy, she reluctantly went, but she felt it put her in direct danger, making her a target, a buck separated from the herd. She secretly asked Nonceba's opinion about it.

Nonceba of course had a different way of seeing it. "I think there is something very powerful about virgins. Have you noticed that most religions put some form of emphasis on virginity? I know that they come across as controlling women's sexuality, but if you choose to be a virgin for as long as you want, the choice is in your hands," she said. "Once it's gone, it's gone, you can never reverse it. But you can choose when to go with whom you want. You can channel your sexual energy into other things until you're ready to change that. Know what I mean?"

What Mvelo liked about Nonceba was that she made sense to her, even though most people thought she was an oddball.

Mvelo went to the virginity testing grounds with clarity in her mind. She was mainly doing it for Zola, yet she also felt she had ownership of herself. And like many girls her age, she was curious to see what and how they tested. She discovered that there were good testers, who were concerned about rampant child abuse and saw testing as the traditional way of solving the problem, but others were drunk with power and the media attention they were getting. Foreign correspondents and rich perverts flocked in with cameras for a flesh circus of unspoiled girls spreading their legs.

Genuine news people were careful not to impose, while the drooling voyeurs used long lenses to focus right on target, just like they did during Umkhosi Wohlanga, the reed dance, where scantily-clad young Zulu maidens present reeds to the Zulu King.

For testing, the old women would line the girls up early in the morning, usually near a river. They would lie down in a row, each with a checker, and open their legs. With two fingers from each hand, the checker would pry open the lips of their little vaginas, looking for an "eye"; the vagina of a virgin is closed up, like a flower bud that looks like an eye. Once she had seen the eye, the checker would come up from between the legs of the virgin and nod to others. There would then be much ululation and joy from the old gogos. The girls got written certificates and were marked with a dot on their foreheads to indicate that they were still pure.

In Mvelo's shantytown, she became known as a virgin girl. Easy prey, like a zebra running among the springboks, marked.

She felt sorry for the girls who had lost their virginity but had to attend the testing for fear of their parents. They sometimes found ways to fool the testers, using a piece of raw liver well placed to make it look as if the hymen was still intact. Some used the chalk from the school blackboard. It was a sad affair because they developed diseases. Testers caught on to the trend and the girls were humiliated in front of the crowds of spectators. Then there were those predators who hunted virgins because a rumor circulated that if an HIV-positive man slept with a virgin he would be cured.

A sexual genocide of children and women began through rape by desperate men. Girls were getting raped left, right, and center. Before Mvelo got home, she learned ways of protecting herself, wiping the white dot from her forehead. She didn't need outside proof to be proud of herself.

Every three months, Mvelo went for a test. The day she stopped going was when one of the older girls was found to be "damaged." This is how the testers referred to girls who were no longer virgins. The girl was about to be married to a traditional church elder who wanted proof that she was "unspoiled."

There was tension in the air. The girl chosen by the traditional leader, who was old enough to be her grandfather, was carrying a load on her shoulders. She didn't want to be married to the old man. She was in love with a young man her own age and she had willingly given herself to him. How could anyone call her damaged? She was in love. If she had been raped, it would be a different thing.

She didn't try to hide it, she just lay there and let the tester spit on her and insult her. Then she began to wail. It was humiliating. After the test, the girl walked away towards the railway tracks, where she lay down and let the train damage and kill her.

Mvelo fainted that day. She was upset and confused by everything. She woke up at home, with the dot of pride still on her forehead. She wiped it off and told Zola that she was never going back.

Most girls in the shacks were damaged from rape. These young girls had trouble on their shoulders. How could they tell their mothers that it was people they trusted, family members, friends of the family, and their "uncles"—their mothers' lovers—who were molesting them?

Mvelo began to resent the whole affair of testing, because they weren't questioning why the girls were "damaged," except when the girl was very young. The rape epidemic was so rampant that some mothers brought in extremely young children as a safety measure against abuse. The "uncles" avoided children that were being tested. They did not want to risk being discovered.

When Mvelo stopped going for the tests, her peers thought she must have been damaged. Why else would she stop going? But she was determined not to let the gossip upset her.

CHAPTER TEN

Mvelo's downward spiral began with the news of a death in 2002. Nonceba's grandmother had died of old age in the States. It was the first time that Mvelo had seen Nonceba so distraught. She was beside herself with grief and Sipho looked on helplessly because he could do nothing to make her feel better. She had to go and bury her grandmother.

It was clear that it wasn't going to be a short trip. She needed to attend to all her grandmother's affairs and spend time grieving. She left, promising to send Mvelo additional math lessons and care packages with all sorts of American goodies through the post. Zola never communicated with Nonceba, out of pride, but she did not interfere with her daughter's friendship with Nonceba. Nonceba sent the packages to Mvelo's school address and continued to communicate with her teachers to ensure that her education did not suffer.

Sipho tried to sell his house. He was lost without Nonceba. He feared that she would not come back, so he started making plans to go to her in America. No one wanted to buy his house in Mkhumbane because Nonceba was rumored to be a witch. That didn't stop Sipho from going to her. He left the house with Mzokhona, his brother, who was very different from Sipho. He was like river debris that moves in whichever direction the river flows, drunk from noon till night. Sipho packed his bags and flew away to join Nonceba.

Nonceba's grandmother Mae had left America for Africa

looking for something she already had. She could trace her roots back to West African slaves and Native American buffalo hunting tribes. And then there were the despicable horrors of the violations of slaves by their masters. It led to her looking less African and more exotic, as though she was from lands unknown. Growing up in the virtually whites-only potato state of Idaho, she did not fit in, so she set out to find a home.

This led her first to the reservations. But watching the devastation of people who were once so close to nature, cramped into a small space in a vast land that they once roamed freely, depressed her. The alcohol and gambling infuriated her. It drained her of hope. So Africa became her destination to search for a place to belong. Her goal was to find the blackest man she could find, who would make her children black, so they would not have the identity crisis that she'd had.

Black girls wouldn't usually give the darkest men the time of day, but Mae was drawn to them like a moth to a light. She found one who was from the proud Tshawe, Phalo, Hintsa, Gambushe, Majola and Thembu, the Xhosa chiefs. She didn't have to go far. She met him on the plane even before touching down in Africa.

He was coming home after studying in the States for some years, helped by scholarships from the missionaries. They were drawn to each other like old souls hit by a sense of déjà vu. Her plan to embark on a pilgrimage from the foot of Mother Africa in Cape Town to her head in Egypt were shelved right there. Gugulethu Hlathi couldn't thank his ancestors enough for bringing him this unexpected beauty.

When the two met, they were the answer to each other's dreams. And then their daughter Zimkitha, "beautiful," Nonceba's mother, was born. They settled in a small tranquil village near the Wild Coast. Zimkitha was the answer to Mae's prayers. Black enough to be viewed as African, with stubborn Native American high cheekbones and hazel eyes, she fit comfortably into the black community. She did not have to endure the cruelty that her mother had experienced. Darker people admired her light skin and treated her well. Children wanted to be her friend, and teachers treated her with extra special care.

It was in her late teens that trouble came knocking. Like a young mule, she couldn't be tamed, and the volatile political uprisings at the time did not help.

Her parents had taught her that she could be anything she wanted to be; she knew no boundaries of rules imposed on blacks. The beautiful Wild Coast was not big enough for her, it choked her free spirit. Events leading to the Soweto uprising saw her cut the apron strings from her protective mother and dictatorial father. She moved to Johannesburg, settling into a cosmopolitan, interracial Hillbrow where she and a bunch of frustrated liberal white youth appointed themselves as civil disobeyers.

Influenced by Gandhi and Martin Luther King Jr., they went around peacefully transgressing. When accosted and forcefully removed from benches marked for whites only, they would sing and dance. Zimkitha loved it, but underneath all this there was serious work going on. They were merely distracting the police from catching on to the young freedom fighters who were mobilizing locally and internationally to set South Africa free.

Part of the reason that Zimkitha started sleeping with Johan Steyn was merely because she had been told not to. She was arrested under the Immorality Act after being caught with him, a well-known Afrikaans dominee's son. Then she found herself in jail, pregnant with Nonceba, Johan's daughter.

She had seen the police coming and she dared Johan to kiss her in front of them. He was terrified at what she was asking him to do. Just when he was about to turn and run, she grabbed hold of him and kissed him deeply. The truth was, she never really loved Johan, her relationship with him was just part of her rebellion.

Johan was timid and Zimkitha was frustrated by this. She suspected that deep down he was still under the spell of apartheid indoctrination. Her relationship with him was the beginning of her downfall. Prison hardened her heart and turned her carefree spirit fearful. Having a child killed her adventurous impulses.

Kissing Johan in public had pressed the buttons she intended to press. The police immediately threw her in jail, and roughed him up, calling him a disgrace for consorting with a *kaffertjie*. But Johan didn't have the courage to stand up for her. He could feel her eyes burning through his back as he walked away, deeply conflicted and embarrassed. She had thought the act would dislodge a freedom fighter latent in him, but she had miscalculated. She had thought he would not let her be arrested with his baby in her belly. When she saw him hang his head in shame, she knew the sting of betrayal. It was no longer a game to disobey the law.

Every step that he took away from her further disconnected him from Zimkitha, and he knew that he had now done something profoundly immoral.

He wrote letters to her compulsively, but he never sent them. In the letters he apologized to her over and over for his weakness and inability to face up to what he knew was wrong.

"What you will never understand is how hard it is to see disappointment in my father's eyes. He is a proud man of God who believes that it is God's will that blacks and whites should never be together. I could never tell him about making you pregnant. I can't bear to lose his love and trust in me. I am the first born of five sons. It would kill me to have my brothers look at me with scorn. I was a good son before leaving Bloemfontein to come to Johannesburg. I believed my father's theories until you sat across from me that day. Your carefree laugh and devil-may-care attitude scared me, but I was drawn to you at the same time. You came into a bar where only the bartenders and not the patrons were black. Yet there you were, a beautiful and tempting black woman. I didn't think you noticed anyone there, let alone me. We were just white faces drinking our beers, and you were with your liberal white pals, stirring up trouble by entering a bar that you knew you were not allowed in. Our shameful secret fantasies were exposed as we blatantly and lustfully stared. Then you and your friends stood up to dance, your hips gyrating as if you were in your own living room. One girl in the group put her arm around your waist as you danced close to each other, your bodies touching. My head began to spin as I watched you in silence. It was the wife of the bar owner who snapped us out of it. She slapped the lust out of her husband, who was practically drooling, and they manhandled you and your friends out of there. They may have removed you from the bar, but not from me. I followed the group until I got a chance to worm my way into your life by making friends with some of your friends, and pretending to be fighting for the same cause. I didn't fool you, though. It took time for you to drop your guard with me. You had breezed into my life and turned me inside out."

Johan wrote these letters to Zimkitha to save himself from going mad. He kept them, in the vain hope that one day he would reunite with her. He fantasized about how she would read them and forgive him.

Before Zimkitha, the only person who had threatened to break his well-molded idea of black people was Sihle, the sole black student who studied medicine with him. Missionaries had pleaded to get him into a university that did not allow blacks in their classrooms, and the lecturers grudgingly taught him, but secretly wished he wasn't as smart as he was because he was proving them wrong about young black minds. Sihle was sensitive to this, but his determination to complete his studies was stronger than any discrimination he had to deal with.

Johan now guiltily remembered how he was one of those who had made Sihle's life hell.

If he ever got that second chance with Zimkitha, would he be brave enough to face up to his father and his family? His thoughts consumed him and he changed into a ghost of his former self. He began operating on autopilot, finishing his medical studies at Wits University, but his mind was barely there. He became addicted to sleeping pills, popping them night after night, as Zimkitha's burning eyes came for him.

When his family suggested Petra, the daughter of another dominee, for a wife, he did not object. He was tired of fighting. He replaced sleeping pills with stronger, numbing drugs. He was a doctor, he kept telling himself, he was not a common addict.

Petra knew she was competing with something powerful for her husband's affection. She sank into her own depression, in a loveless, childless marriage. She took comfort in the fact that she was married to a doctor, with a family that appeared to love God. She dared not scratch the surface. Things lurking under the peaceful façade were too frightening.

Zimkitha broke when they threw her into a dark, silent cell and left her there for months. The only sound was the dripping tap, day in and day out. She had grown desperate and had made a plan, which she waited to execute. On the morning that she went into labor, she grabbed hold of the hand that popped in to drop her one meal of the day. She sank her teeth in and locked her jaw like a pit bull. The screams of agony from the warden brought others running. They opened the cell and were confronted by the stinging smell of Zimkitha's stale urine, and the horror of blood in her mouth. She looked like a crazed animal, her overgrown, unkempt bushy hair covering most of her face.

Right there her water broke. They were shocked into action. While some tended to the bitten woman warder, others busied themselves assisting her to give birth to Nonceba. A new life has a way of making hardened hearts forget about everything else.

Zimkitha decided to name her golden baby Nonceba, "mother of sympathy."

The baby became her ticket to freedom, but the experience left her too damaged to carry on. She left Johannesburg and went back to be with her mother in the Eastern Cape. Her father had gone out of his mind with worry when he heard about her arrest and had joined the struggle and led strikes. He had been shot and killed for fighting for her release. Then Mae's talk of returning to America began, but Zimkitha simply refused. Her mother had told her the stories about how she had suffered there, and she didn't want to be in another country that was spiteful to her.

She wasn't coping with the baby and with the continued killings of freedom fighters. She became listless. Her spark was gone and the fight had drained out of her. On Nonceba's first birthday, as they were blowing out the candles on the little girl's cake and clapping to her joyful, childish squeals, the radio announced a train massacre. The announcer talked of black on black violence, but Zimkitha knew it was so much more than that. Hers and Mae's faces fell in dismay. They looked at each other and Nonceba, young as she was, sensed the change of mood and began to cry. Her grandmother picked her up and walked about trying to calm her.

Zimkitha began to tremble. The frustration of it was choking her. She couldn't breathe. Mae held her close and rocked her until she stopped shaking. "I don't know why I thought we could win this. I don't know why we even fought this," she told her mother through her tears.

Young Nonceba was looking at both of them with big sad eyes. Mae switched off the radio and they listened to the sound of the ocean humming nearby.

Zimkitha waited for her mother to take Nonceba with her to the craft circle where Mae worked with community women making baskets.

Then she calmly walked into the waves.

CHAPTER ELEVEN

Things turned when Sipho joined Nonceba in the States. He always knew that she was a contained fire that would consume flesh and lick bones clean if she was given the chance. When she met him at O'Hare Airport in Chicago, the cold February air hit him in the face like a strong fist of that beautiful legend, Muhammad Ali. He wanted to turn around and take the next plane back to sunny Africa, but Nonceba was there, bright with joy at meeting up with him again.

He only had to look into Nonceba's eyes to know that whatever it was that he would face in America, he would stay, because she had his heart. She told him about her grandmother's funeral. To distract herself from the pain of losing Mae, she had started working in her old law firm again. She said it was just while she was figuring things out about coming back to Africa.

Her apartment was large, with windows that overlooked Lake Michigan. Sipho was amazed that she had left behind such a good life to be with him in Mkhumbane. He laughed long and hard about that.

When he arrived, she made a barbeque at a friend's house in Oak Park. To get there, they took the L train, crisscrossing above the city through the maze of tall buildings and passing the magnificent home of the Chicago Tribune.

Sipho loved Oak Park. He told the gathering of friends stories of Mkhumbane and Skwiza's *shebeen*, and about the first time he had taken Nonceba there. As he spoke, a realization dawned on him, that he belonged in Mkhumbane. He carried on talking, but he knew then that he would not last in Chicago if Nonceba decided to stay in America permanently.

The cold was freezing hairs inside his nostrils and something inside of him was losing balance. He was not used to walking on ice and he kept falling and hitting his ass hard against the cold ground. Then his tailbone started giving him pain.

He laughed and kept drawing strangers towards him. Unlike the *tsotsis* in Mkhumbane, these people were different. They didn't want anything from him. They didn't need his money, and they didn't bask in the light of him being a lawyer. They were lawyers themselves. They had PhDs at the end of their names and they engaged with each other at an intellectual level.

Sipho held his own comfortably among these intelligent people. It fascinated them, because they could never have imagined this from a real "Aaafrican." But he became exhausted with the mask he had to wear. He missed Skwiza's and indulging in mundane small talk about the Soweto soccer derby, his brain soaked in whiskey.

He loved the view of Lake Michigan. It was shiny at night. But the neon lights frustrated him because they added an unnatural golden light onto the water's surface. He wanted the silver lights of the moon that he was used to where he grew up in eMpendle. Moonlight made everything beautiful to him. He felt spiritually connected to the moon. Lake Michigan gave him comfort.

He struggled to find work and it threw him into a crisis that he never thought possible. The problem for him was that he was a man being supported by a woman. For the first time in his life, he felt the fears of women who had to depend on men. He began to understand why women would do anything to keep their men. He thought of Zola and how different she was; how much courage it must have taken to leave him. Fear gripped his heart like the icy cold Chicago winter air. His laughter was no longer deep and joyful.

He began to feel insecure around Nonceba, who was out climbing the merciless corporate ladder. She worked day in and day out, with double the intensity that she had when she was with Sipho in Mkhumbane, and she became short with him. She had no time to spend with him.

The cold was taking its toll on Sipho too and he fell into a deep depression. He slept all day, hating the thought of waking up to another grey sky. He stopped taking baths, changing his clothes, and brushing his teeth. This put a nail in the coffin of their intimate lives. "I don't know what to do, he's not the man I fell in love with." Nonceba was in tears on the phone talking to one of her friends. "He's a shell of himself. He repulses me now. It pains me to say it but, this man who used to make me feel like a queen, now I dread coming home to him."

Sipho had become so clingy and insecure that he listened to her conversations from the bedroom that only he used now. He wept silently on hearing what he had suspected, but dreaded to admit.

He woke up the next day after Nonceba had gone to work, and looked into the mirror, and what he saw reflected back at him was a picture of his brother, Mzokhona, the river debris. His hair was unkempt, his teeth were coated with a yellow film, and his tongue was furry. He sobbed under a hot shower. The water revived him, then he scrubbed himself and Nonceba's house clean.

He waited for her to come back to tell her that he was going home. He wanted to be where his feet were planted on the ground. This strange place left him feeling wobbly, like a child learning to walk. Like an exile, he could no longer laugh. A heavy rock sat on his chest, making it hard for him to breathe. Inhaling the air was painful. It felt as if his lungs were being assaulted with ice. He wanted to get back to his work, practicing law and helping those who were on the periphery of society in Mkhumbane and the neighboring shacks.

It was late in the evening when she finally got back. "I knew this day would come," she said.

He ran out of words, and she cried.

Then, for the first time in a long time, they talked like they used to. She apologized for getting sucked back into her old workaholic ways. She had done some thinking of her own and knew that it was also time for her to return to South Africa. But it was clear to them both that it was time to go their separate ways.

"Just do me one favor," she said, wiping away her tears. "I will be going to my grandfather's village when I get to South Africa. Don't try to contact me. I'll contact you when I'm ready to face you as a friend and not as a lover."

She felt that she had unfinished business in the country where her mother had taken her life, her grandfather had died a violent death, and possibly she still had a living, breathing father.

They fell asleep on the carpet, spooning like the children of the shacks who share a single bed.

CHAPTER TWELVE

Sipho's house was a sight when he got back to Mkhumbane. In the couple of years that he had been gone, his brother had managed to break everything. The television had a hole in it, the microwave had been sold, and the electricity was unpaid and had been disconnected. Half his towels and linen, bought by Nonceba, had been sold. The rooms were rented out to the strays of the township. They were using paraffin, primus stoves or good old-fashioned firewood, campfire style, to cook on the floor. The whole house smelled of a mixture of paraffin and wood smoke. The walls were black with soot. Even the bathroom was being used as a sleeping area for two homeless children.

Sipho's brother had the telltale signs that drinking had taken a toll on him. He looked older than Sipho by a number of years, although he was ten years younger. It was hard to work out if he was smiling or sneering when he revealed his red gums and greenish teeth. He was surprised by Sipho's unannounced return and scared of how he would react to the state of the place.

Sipho was shocked by what he saw. He headed to the only family he knew, Zola and Mvelo, at their shack. They were still there, and their home was clean and welcoming.

Mvelo thought she was dreaming when she lifted her eyes and saw a tall, familiar figure walking towards her. A scream of joy lifted from her chest and rang out across the shack valley. "It's him," she shouted, "he is back. Ma, Sipho is back!"

She ran towards him, crashing against his broad chest. His laughter rang like music in her ears. Zola stood at the door, leaning heavily against it, trying to keep her face neutral but she couldn't suppress a smile. She didn't want to show too much excitement. The history between them had taught her to be guarded, but the love she felt for Sipho remained.

Nonceba was not with him, but Mvelo settled for the fact that at least he was back. She still enjoyed the care packages that Nonceba sent.

Sipho regaled them with stories, showered them with presents from America, and before they knew it, it was deep into the middle of the night. The excitement of it all finally got the better of Mvelo, who gave in to a sweet sleep. Sipho and Zola surrendered to the pull of familiarity with each other's bodies, for old time's sake.

It was a beautiful Saturday morning when Mvelo woke with Sipho and Zola under one roof. She began to nurse abandoned hopes that perhaps they would be a family again.

Zola had a small tune on her lips as she prepared breakfast for them, like she always had when she was happy. Sipho and Mvelo looked at each other and smiled. It made them happy hearing Zola singing like that.

After finishing their porridge, they all went back to Sipho's house. Zola took two buckets, a scrubbing brush, Jeyes Fluid and liquid soap to help him clean the house.

His brother had seen the writing on the wall and told all his "tenants" to disappear, threatening them with Nonceba. "You better scram, the great witch of Mkhumbane is back. Find other shelters because this one is no longer available."

Bringing up Nonceba's name was the magic word. They disappeared faster than cockroaches at the sight of light. Some didn't know her in person, but the stories were enough to make them pack what they could and go.

Sipho sighed with relief when he saw that they did not resist their eviction. His brother winked at him, pleased with his own quick thinking. There was no stiff formal apology between the two. Sipho took a hosepipe and sprayed him down and playfully chased him around as he sputtered. Life went on. He was Sipho's leech, and Sipho obliged as part of that unquestioned family obligation. They were brothers.

Zola and Mvelo spent the weekend cleaning, scrubbing down the walls. Sipho's friends from the tavern joined in when they heard that he had come back alone without the witch. His brother, of course, wormed his way out of everything. He developed "crippling flu," and just as the house got back to its old shining glory the following week, he recovered miraculously with an unquenchable thirst for a "cold one." After he was refreshed, he had enough strength to start teasing Zola again. "Now that my brother is back, you know who I am, don't you? You wouldn't give me the time of day before. Don't get comfortable, Nonceba is coming back." Sipho shot him a warning look, but he wouldn't stop.

When Zola packed up after the cleanup, and got ready to return home, Sipho was surprised. He had assumed they would be moving back with him. Zola had entertained no such idea.

"But what about the other night?" he said.

"What about it?"

"Well, can't we forget about the past and try again?" he asked, exasperated.

She laughed and said, "I see things haven't changed a bit with you. Please take us back to where we belong. I have helped you with your house; now please take me back to mine."

She had recovered from Sipho's charms. She had been surprised beyond belief when he'd showed up like that. In her state of shock, she had done things she'd vowed never to do again with Sipho.

A few days of thinking while cleaning had jogged her memory and brought her back to her senses.

Sipho was taken aback. He didn't know what he had really expected. He just knew that he needed someone to make him feel like a man again, someone to adore him like she and Mvelo used to. The fact is, they did, but they also had their own lives that did not have him at the center. He discovered that Zola was still soft and gentle on the outside, but pure steel on the inside.

She was no longer bitter towards him. In fact, it was quite the opposite. She was happy to see him, and made it known, but she wouldn't let him into her life as a provider and rescuer again. She no longer needed his protection. Life in the shacks had taught her to stiffen her spine and get on with surviving and providing for her daughter. Sipho was no longer the god he had been to her back then.

It drove him crazy. He was feeling lost and vulnerable. He wanted Zola to anchor him, to ease him back to the old, assured self that he was before he began depending on somebody else's salary. He still couldn't promise Zola that there wouldn't be others competing for his affections. But at that moment, she was the one he wanted.

Zola's refusal drove him into the arms of many desperate Mkhumbane floozies. He called it sexual healing. He needed to affirm his manliness and balance himself again. From a distance, Zola watched with disappointment. Even Mvelo knew then that what he was doing was wrong.

She was growing up and she had come to believe that there were certain expectations when someone said they loved you. It didn't seem right just to spread the love all over the place. Also, at school they were learning about the spread of HIV-AIDS, and she was worried for Sipho.

He went back to his old law practice and continued to play savior to those with eviction notices, and the *tsotsis* of Mkhumbane were overjoyed to have him back.

His insatiable longing for the affections of women caused many a catfight at his office. He had liaisons with several secretaries at the firm, who couldn't resist the charms of a powerful lawyer. Such rendezvous don't remain secret for long. Some of these young, wide-eyed secretaries thought he may be a ladder to better things in the firm; some were seduced by his charisma. He drank more than usual to try and forget Nonceba and the sting of rejection by Zola. He worked during the day, slept with the secretaries when the urge called, and drank at night with his friends in the *shebeen*.

CHAPTER THIRTEEN

Sipho was nursing a humongous hangover when Joy, his personal secretary, showed up at his house looking like she was heavily drugged. It was mid-morning on a Saturday and her big eyes looked glazed and her lips were dry, as though she hadn't eaten in days. It was only then that he noticed how much weight she had lost. A chill ran through his body as she took a seat next to him on his veranda. Then she dropped a bombshell that left him feeling dazed.

"I am pregnant with your child," she sighed heavily. She wasn't happy. She was much younger than Sipho and had been planning to study. She didn't want to remain a secretary for the rest of her life. She felt stupid for falling for the charms of her boss.

Sipho's ears rang. In the back of his mind, he had always known this day would come; he was reckless when it came to women. His sharp brain seemed to shrink and turn upside down when his lower regions inflated. To those like Nonceba, who insisted on a condom, he obliged. But he always seemed to assume that it was the responsibility of the woman to deal with prevention measures for pregnancies and, God forbid, diseases.

The stricken Joy made Sipho feel guilty. He knew that he was in the wrong. He was older, and she was in a subordinate position. He held her close. "Please don't cry, baby, I am here. I am not going anywhere. Whatever you decide to do, I am here for you."

Her body stiffened. "What do you mean, whatever I decide to do?" She extracted herself from his arms to look him in the eyes with guarded fury.

Sipho felt helpless. "I mean, if you want to keep the baby or not," he said hesitantly, pointing to her stomach that seemed rather flat now.

"Oh no, I was not alone in this. You were there grunting sweet nothings when you planted your dirty little tadpoles. Now you want me to make this decision alone!"

She was angry at herself because she knew that she wasn't the only woman in his life. But by the time she found out about the others, it was too late. She was hooked, in love beyond logic, and she couldn't bring herself to dump him. She loved him and hated him at the same time. "I am telling you now that I am not getting rid of this baby, and I expect you to come home to my parents to explain yourself."

The submissive Joy was gone. Sipho stood there, shocked by this transformation. His head was throbbing from the previous day's whiskey. He simply nodded, wanting to get rid of her so that he could get some sleep.

After a month of tension and dirty looks from Joy, who spent considerable time heaving in the toilet, things turned south. She had gone for routine tests and her last visit to the clinic brought dark news. Not only was she pregnant, she was also HIV-positive. When she heard this, she fainted in the counselor's office.

The counselor used the telephone number Joy wrote on the form to call Sipho. "Sir, we need you to please come to our rooms as soon as possible. Your girlfriend is having some complications."

Sipho's heart flipped, skipping beats as he felt fear spread throughout his body. Getting a call from this kind of clinic turns everyone's knees into jelly. The ride to Addington

Hospital seemed to be on automatic pilot. His legs became heavy, each step labored, like a slow motion scene in an action movie.

He never smoked, but at that moment he craved a long drag of a cigarette. He stood in front of the counselor's door but didn't knock. He had an overwhelming urge to turn around and run as fast as he could.

But the door opened before he could do that. The counselor had a kind face. She looked at him across the doorway, and smiled a sad little smile, recognizing his fear. She was familiar with it by now. She was trained to calm people down and shift their minds from doom to questions of how they could manage the disease in their bloodstream.

Joy was sleeping peacefully on the office floor with her shoes off. By now a small bump was showing on her tummy, but her frame remained slender. "Joy came in for a test. I had to call you because I see that you are the father of the baby she is carrying. She will need your help to get home. She's resting now. Let's give her a little time and then you can take her home."

"What tests? What were the results? Why did she faint?" Sipho asked all these questions without giving the counselor space to explain.

"Well, it is up to Joy to explain to you when she wakes."

As if on cue, Joy woke up with a start, looking confused. When her eyes registered Sipho, she went for him, punching him in the face and screaming at him. "You are poison, you have killed me. I am dying of a disease I never thought would reach me." She was spitting venom like a disturbed cobra. "I thought you were a clean, decent man, but you were whoring all over town. Look at us now. Don't even deny it, I know it was you. I was fine before you came along."

Then she collapsed on a chair and cried some more.

Her weave was disheveled. She looked like a demented woman. The counselor handed her a brown paper bag to breathe into to calm herself.

Sipho sat there, his face throbbing from her punches. *Surrender,* the voice in his head kept repeating. He had to surrender himself to the news. He calmly asked the counselor if he could take a test of his own. He knew it was a formality because every part of his being knew he had to have it. He didn't have enough fingers and toes to count the women he had been with. Finally, he took exhausted Joy home with him.

After all her ranting, she simply shut down, and fell into a fitful sleep.

For Sipho, it was the longest night of his life as he waited till the next day for the results. Images of his numerous women flashed through his mind, but it was the thought of Zola that brought a lump in his throat.

By morning, his pillow was soaked with the salty tears of his regrets.

During the counseling, he could hear the words coming from the kind looking nurse in front of him, but he felt as if he was underwater. Although he expected the result to be positive, confirmation made him sob for the lives he had managed to ruin.

CHAPTER FOURTEEN

When Sipho came to visit them, Mvelo was happy to see him as usual. But she was surprised when this time, instead of letting her see him off, he asked Zola to walk him to his car.

A dark cloud hung over their shack from that day onwards. Zola's silence became intense again. She visited the clinic regularly, and her demands for attending church became urgent. She and Mvelo became exemplary devotees.

One day she sat Mvelo down and reminded her of the day Sipho came from America. With hot tears pouring from her eyes, she said she had exposed herself to HIV that day. She had never been the one to talk with Mvelo about sex openly, but that day she spoke to her about having not used protection with Sipho since his return. Ever since she had broken up with Sipho, she had not been friendly with men.

Mvelo felt a heavy stone take a seat in her heart. She hated Sipho for making Zola cry again. It seemed to her that her mother's destiny revolved around Sipho. It took her time to be able to look him in the eye again.

Zola displayed the classic symptoms of someone who was confronting matters of life and death. She told Mvelo she better hurry up and get over her hate because life was leaving her behind. It was the fear of the disease that made Mvelo so angry. She hated Sipho for infecting her mother and for breaking up with Nonceba. She hated Joy because she wanted a scapegoat; she wanted to blame her for the misery that had come into their lives.

The day that Zola told her about her HIV status, Mvelo took a long walk through the maze of shacks, without purpose, just trying to get away from her tears. A protruding, sharp piece of corrugated iron scratched her leg and she bled. But instead of pain, she felt a calming, warm sensation, and the sight of the blood gave her all sorts of thoughts about how to cure Zola. Under the moonlight, she stared at her blood rushing out of her body and she felt a release from the pressure that was building inside of her. She looked at her clean blood and thought it could be possible. Some clever doctor could drain out the infected blood from Zola and inject Mvelo's blood into her.

Now, on some nights, after listening to Zola quietly crying herself to sleep, Mvelo would wake up and cut her flesh with a razor, to see the blood and feel that calming feeling again.

Two months after receiving the news, Joy swallowed Jeyes Fluid and was found in the fetal position in the office toilet. Her suicide note simply read: "Wolves in sheep's clothing who pretend to be lovers... You might win some but you just lost one."

The unfinished business began aggressively eating away at Sipho. He deteriorated quickly after Joy's death. His legs refused to carry him. His weight dropped off, leaving his tall frame looking shockingly weak. Zola and a group of home-based care volunteers visited him where he was holed up in his house, feasting on self-pity. They cleaned the house together, but Zola insisted on preserving his dignity by being the only one who changed his clothes and sponge-bathed him.

Mvelo simply shut down. She wanted to erase him from her memory. She was angry with Zola and banned her from talking about him to her.

The rumor mill was spinning. People spoke in whispers. It was then that Mvelo dreamed of him crying and drowning. In the dream, she frantically tried to pull him out, but he let go of her hand. "If you ever believed anything about me, believe this, I love you," he said and he let go, smiling. She woke up shaking and soaking wet. She had to see him at least one last time because, even deep in her rage, she knew that she still loved him as the only father she had ever had.

When she told Zola about the dream, Zola sat her down and said: "I know you think I am foolish for doing what I am doing but I tell you that if I hold a grudge against he who has done me wrong, I would die quickly and leave you behind. And I am not ready for that. And as for you carrying hate at such a young age, I am afraid it will weigh you down and you will let life pass you by. It is not for Sipho that I do the things that I do, it is for me. It is to keep me healthy and alive with a purpose. Besides, we both really did love him once; that love doesn't just die. I think it is stifled deep in your little chest. That's why you are dreaming things now."

As Zola spoke, Mvelo saw that her mother had really shifted the way she thought about things. She seemed calmer and wiser.

Mvelo visited Sipho after months of avoiding him, and she gasped from shock. He was a shadow of his former self. His eyes filled with tears when he saw her, all grown-up and tall, a version of Zola. They didn't say a word. Mvelo sat by his bed and they just looked at each other. They talked with their eyes and absorbed each other. At that moment, Mvelo shifted the protective stone she had in her heart and allowed the pain and frustration to scrub her clean and make her feel again.

Sipho became weaker physically, but his spirit remained. On good days, he still managed to make them laugh.

He gave the house to his brother, the river debris. Maybe if Mzokhona had a place to settle he would change, Sipho hoped. His practice was sold for next to nothing to his partners. Since he was not married, his affairs were handled by his mother with the help of his lawyer friends. He agreed to everything, but he stubbornly refused her offer to move him back home to eMpendle. He chose the hospice at Addington Hospital instead.

While he was there, he made the nurses laugh and gave comic relief to the other patients with his jokes. Some days were better; others unbearable. He sank in and out of melancholy, especially when the topic of Nonceba or Zola came up. Maybe it was guilt that ravaged him more than the illness itself.

The hospice was his last home. He never got to face Nonceba. One day they were all laughing, he was telling Zola a joke and the intensity of his laughter went up a notch, then his heart gave in. He died laughing.

CHAPTER FIFTEEN

Sipho's life affirming jokes had a way of softening even the hardest of hearts. He had been a shining light in the middle of sickness and death at the hospice. The staff nicknamed him Patch Adams, even though he wasn't a physician, because he seemed to want to cure with laughter.

When Zola realized he was gone, she walked slowly to the window. She wanted to see if anything had changed outside, if the world was mourning him. But the grey clouds stared back at her, unaffected. The ocean still playfully teased the tourists, as hawkers shouted the prices of their trinkets. The ladies of the night, now trading in broad daylight, took drags on their cigarettes and seduced the passers-by as always. Drug pushers exchanged Durban Poison for money with clean but frustrated citizens in suits. The blind man with the voice of an angel still sat on the corner singing "Summertime," except the living wasn't easy.

Zola began to rant incessantly at God and the ancestors. Then she made a selfless supplication for Sipho, giving God and the ancestors a list of things he liked, starting with the moon. "He loved the moon," she said, "welcome him with the moon. And he loved women, ancient ones, make sure they are plentiful at his reception. Then the children. Let there be sounds of laughing children; that will make him happy. Oh yes, and music. Not the sad kind, but the drums and raw voices of African maidens. Send them with Mfaz' Omnyama, the *maskandi* legend, strumming his guitar."

Zola had always known that she loved Sipho, even with all the hardship and hurt he had caused her. She couldn't stand his women, but on that day she gave him up freely and selflessly.

Mvelo just broke down and cried; she was relieved. Finally, it was the day of his forgiveness.

His grumpy old hag of a mother was mortified when she heard his final wish that he had conveyed to Zola. It was just like Sipho, a joker till the last. He had asked for all the women at his funeral to remove their undergarments and place them on his coffin. Under no circumstances was his mother willing to announce this, of course, but it did give Zola a laugh. Both Sipho's request and his mother's reaction. Zola had often wondered how it was that Sipho came from this prune-faced woman.

His mother was determined that Zola would not get to smell a cent of the money that he had wanted to leave her. The old woman was not going to tell her that he had pleaded and begged that his money and the house should go to Zola and Mvelo, but she would not hear of it. "Under the tail of the donkey," is what she said to herself. She was fuming that her son had chosen this young, unmarried city girl to inherit his money over her. His words were like a spear to her heart. It reminded her of Sipho's father who was swallowed by Ndongazibovu, the red walls of Johannesburg, and its young girls with curves she did not have.

When they all gathered in the hall to bid him farewell, the men were bewildered. "*uSipho ubeyisoka lamanyala.*" He was a man who had a way with women. How does one man have so many women loving him?

"Eish, my bro, I mean all his yesterdays are here," his drunkard brother said out loud, causing laughter among the somber men. "What is it that he had that we don't have?"

They scratched their heads, knowing that their yesterdays wouldn't even speak to them alive, let alone come to their funerals. Some stood in a stupor. Others drooled openly at the sight and smell of Sipho's yesterdays, todays, and tomorrows: tall and short, young and old, fat and thin, they were beautiful in their collective sadness.

The sun was out and the sky was clear, the bluest blue. It was serene like the clarity of his mind at the end of his life. After they had viewed his body, the sky collapsed on them. It rained fiercely, large refreshing drops. The earth and the women soaked it up. The soil smelled delicious. Women stood in it and stretched out their arms for it to kiss them. They kicked off their high heels and, barefooted, they laughed and cried as the men carefully lowered him down into his final resting place, the greedy earth.

Mvelo desperately said a prayer, hoping it would spare her mother, this insatiable earth that continues to swallow without chewing and greedily gorges itself.

And just as Sipho would have wished it, like the screech of an old-fashioned record with a needle being pulled across it, a cacophony of sirens interrupted the sad music that had accompanied the coffin into the earth, and disturbed the ceremony. The bikes of four traffic cops escorted a distinguished-looking, black Mercedes that came to a standstill in the parking lot. The music stopped as everyone turned to watch, and Sipho's mother let out a surprised cry as a lady about her age but taller, well-groomed, and fitter, stepped out. She was wearing a bright red dress and a hat with a long shiny black feather of some exotic bird; expensive pearls adorned her ears and neck.

A chauffeur in black stood to attention alongside the car. She shooed away the traffic cops on motorbikes that had been clearing traffic for her. They touched their hats, nodded, and were off. Then she glided towards everyone assembled there, chest out, back straight, shoulders steady and each step precise. She looked as though she had been a ballet dancer in her youth.

The crowd was silent as she got closer. She went straight to Sipho's mother and demanded: "Harriet, what do you think you are doing? How can you bury Danny without telling me? After everything I have done for you, you decide to cut me out like this?" She was so angry, she was shaking. She spoke perfect isiZulu and there were murmurs of surprise from the crowd.

What came next shocked everyone. MaMdletshe squared up to her. "His name is Sipho, not Danny, Julia, and I don't owe you anything. But before you accuse me of being ungrateful, you should know that I did come to your house to notify you and your security guards chased me away."

This was Julia who had been Sipho's mother's employer for fifteen years, and there had long been bitter rivalry between the two for Sipho's affections. Julia had spoken to him in English, excluding his mother from their conversations, but now that maMdletshe was on home ground, she was determined to have her say. "You tried to steal my son by turning him against me, filling his head with your eccentricities, but you failed, Julia. You failed, and Sipho, my son, took his name back and came back to me."

Julia had nurtured Sipho academically, paying for his university education, so she felt some claim on his memory. "I saw that he had talent and all I wanted to do was help the boy to fulfill his dreams. The school here in the village taught him the rudiments, Harriet, but after he passed Matric somebody had to help him. You are the one who walked off in a huff. I was the one who insisted that he visited you. What do you want from me?"

◄—◇—►

"Do you know that you nearly made me lose my mind when you tried to take him overseas with you? Why would you want to steal my child?" maMdletshe demanded.

"But I didn't! I paid his tuition and I left because I couldn't stand this country and all its bullshit," Julia snapped.

Now it was Sipho's mother's turn to cackle. "But you came back, didn't you? There is no place like home, Julia. You missed us over there where they say there is no sun for months or maids to clean your toilets. You must have been miserable."

Julia let out an exasperated breath, flounced around, and with a flip of her hands, instructed the men to take the coffin out. They obeyed immediately, as they were used to doing with Madams.

"Danny had a free spirit, Harriet, he belonged to no one," Julia said, and then dissolved into a mess of tears.

Sipho's mother softened, took Lady Julia's hand, and led her to the coffin, where they stood silently together for a moment.

And then music began. But it wasn't a sad funeral melody. It was the voices of the maidens that Sipho loved.

The mourners from another funeral, burying someone next to Sipho's tomb, were Zionists and they had drums with them. When they heard the maidens singing, they joined in and beat their drums, as a taxi passed by with a song of Mfaz' Omnyama blasting out, and Sipho's party broke out clapping, singing and jigging.

Mvelo looked at her mother and saw satisfaction; Zola's prayer had been answered, there was a celebratory funeral for her Sipho. Then Mvelo looked at the old, white lady who had stood up to Sipho's mother and she decided that she liked her. This Lady Julia was spoiled, and expected the world to serve her, but it had taken guts for her to come here today.

The thing that nobody knew was the real bond that existed

between her and Sipho. She was the one who had introduced him to forbidden fruit. She had snuck up on him in the shower one day, and what followed had turned him into the confident man who had made it a lifetime's pursuit to make women swoon.

When his mother decided to stop working for Julia, he had disobeyed her for the first time by refusing to come home with her. It had broken her heart, and was tough on Sipho, but he wanted the luxuries that came with living in a city. The thought of moving back to the rural areas was too much for him. He had dug in his heels, and promised to visit his mother.

Now, as the funeral party prepared to move back to the hospice, to continue reminiscing about Sipho with those who had been too sick to attend, Julia made her final exit from his life. The shining lights on her Mercedes faded away as she was driven back to her mansion in Kloof.

That night Mvelo listened to her mother reminiscing about Sipho with Dora, their neighbor, outside their shack after the funeral. Zola liked sitting outside in the moonlight on summer evenings. She unwrapped the silver foil covering the muffins they had taken from the funeral for supper, and gave one to Dora. She didn't take one for herself. This was the way they were able to save for the next meal, by skipping one if they didn't feel too hungry. She called out to Mvelo to take the rest inside. "It's bedtime, Mvelo. You had better get some sleep. I'll be out here with Dora."

Mvelo heard her mother tell Dora that even with all the women who had come to the funeral, Sipho was not some mythical saint of a man. "Lady Charmer, yes, he made the panties drop, but saintly, far from it," she chuckled sadly. "I loved Sipho since I was a teenager, but I am a grown woman now and, as much as I worshipped him then, as his other women did, he was a fallible man with many faults, some of which had fatal consequences. His charm left many women hovering on the thin line between love and hate for him. Isn't it just the way, that the ones we love most can hurt us the most.

"He had that skill of reading women and taking on the role that he thought would appeal to each one. He was a provider and protector to me, to my daughter he was a father, and with Nonceba, he was hopelessly in love and very vulnerable. He had a never-ending need to be loved. Like all his women, I wasn't immune. I was devoted to him, but I wasn't blinded. I sensed his sadness. All that love at his disposal, yet no one really knew him. He used to say, with each new woman he felt like a virgin again because he was encountering new curves, new scents, and new movements."

Zola and Dora laughed softly like girls exchanging secrets.

"He was not the best looking man. It was his presence that left women confused and helpless." Zola seemed to be struggling to find the right words to explain her lover. "When his friends asked, he always said, 'The woman who turned me into a man was not a fumbling, blushing girl. I was a fumbling boy and she was worldly, like old wine.' His eyes would shine as the guys hung on to every word. Then he would take a swig of his whiskey. 'Women are mysterious creatures,' he would say, 'with subtleties that you have to study closely. My first taught me how to treat a lady until she is butter in my warm hands. I don't make them scream, with me they roar like beautiful, powerful cats of the jungle. Some cry their eyes out and speak in tongues because it becomes a religious experience for them.' Then he would laugh like a cat himself that had got all the cream."

This talk of sex horrified Mvelo. It was a side of her mother that she knew nothing about. She felt guilty for eavesdropping, but remained glued to the spot. From the crack in the doorway, she could see Zola. She looked down as she spoke to Dora, who mostly offered no comments but simply smiled and nodded, as if to say, "Yes, I know what you mean." Mvelo was happy that her mother had someone adult to speak to. Dora was a picture of compassion.

She watched her mother smooth her black skirt with her hands. After a long, thoughtful silence, she said, "You know, Sipho was terrified to just be himself. He never trusted any of his women to love him regardless. It was only on his sickbed that he tried to let go of his masks, but even then it was only to me and my daughter." Mvelo had never heard her mother be so personal with anyone before. Then Zola told Dora about how Sipho had asked her to finish him off if he ever got to the point of losing his bearings.

A few days before he died, he had grabbed her arm and held on. His strength surprised her. "When I start shitting myself and I can't talk, or recognize you, you have to do something for me. Let me rest, let me go. Use a pillow, a knife, or anything that will put me out of this misery. I have caused you so much pain. I don't deserve your kindness. But if you have ever loved me, I ask this of you, do not let me live another minute when I become the living dead," he whispered, his eyes looking into hers, feverish and determined, willing her to say yes.

Zola recoiled in shock, every ounce of her body rejecting this curse of a dying man's wish. But looking into his eyes, she knew she had to lie and say yes. Her response brought a smile to his face. "That's my girl," he said, squeezing her hand. She smiled back with tears in her eyes, and it was sealed.

She sat there feeling close to him again, like in the old days. He seemed free and relieved. Then he began to get better and hope was resuscitated in them. But life is cruel like that, like caressing the chicken before twisting its neck.

Zola said his death was like being riddled with bullets by a firing squad. "I think I temporarily lost my mind, my heart was ripped out of me." Tears didn't come for her now, but her inner cries were audible to Dora's sympathetic ear.

CHAPTER SIXTEEN

After Johan had sunk further and further into depression and taken a near-fatal overdose of prescription drugs, Petra surprised him one day and announced in her business-like way that she was going to begin a search for his child. "We have to find her," she said. "I can see that it is killing you and I don't want to lose you."

Johan fell in love with his wife that day, after all the years of their empty marriage, and the two of them became a team in the hunt for his daughter.

They had tried to find Nonceba for some years now but it had proved fruitless. All he knew was that Zimkitha had a surname that meant bush or forest when translated into English. He also knew that she came from the coast, but he was not sure which coast, east or west.

On a hunch, they moved to Durban, partly hoping to find a lead pointing to Nonceba, and partly to help with the scourge of HIV-AIDS that was ravaging KwaZulu-Natal. They moved into a modest house in Manor Gardens and worked with youth encouraging them to choose responsible lifestyles. Unlike their neighbors, their home was unfenced, and left to fate should the *tsotsis* pay them a visit.

Johan was a different man after coming out of his dark depression. The thing that he was most afraid of, being rejected by his family, had already happened and he had survived it. In fact, he had been liberated by it. He was no longer confined by his father's inflexible teaching, no longer searching for his father's approval. He felt free, with a new surge of purpose, and so he and Petra threw their energies into helping to build a new South Africa.

Although they had by now stopped actively looking for the young woman whose name they didn't know, they both still hoped that fate would bring them together.

Petra's longing for a child of her own remained a throbbing wound that could never heal. For a while it had got her down and made her depressed, especially when nature decided to shut down her monthly reassurances that it was still a possibility. The finality of it cut through her hopes and broke her heart. Their plans of adopting remained talk. It never came to fruition because they were so busy. Johan, on the other hand, still hoped that one day he would meet his own flesh and blood. He kept looking at young women in their thirties, hoping to see the fierce eyes of Zimkitha looking back at him.

Petra threw herself into helping young women with bigger problems than her own, and this took the focus away from her private pain. The Bible remained her source of comfort.

They spent most of their days in the neighboring shacks doing home visits for those too sick to get to hospitals. They learned about the dignity and resourcefulness of the shack dwellers. Unattractive as their shacks were on the outside, the interiors showed incredible innovation and survival skills. The walls were beautifully covered with decorative wallpaper made from magazines and gift wrap. Almost all had TV sets, some running on vehicle batteries. The shacks that were situated closer to the suburbs often had illegal electrical wires connecting them to the city's electricity grid.

Petra was constantly amazed by how shack dwellers made a plan and lived their lives to the full. On weekends, radios were on full blast, with people dancing, swaying their hips this way and that to the music. If one of them surrendered to death, the community got together and offered assistance where they could bury one of their own with dignity.

But there were some things that did not make sense to her. The fights that broke out during the drinking sessions, the constant incidents of children losing their innocence through brutal rape, and the growing number of children left to fend for themselves.

The two of them would come back from their visits feeling exhausted, silent during their drive home, with each of them focused on their own thoughts about the day. Sometimes it would be a feeling of helplessness at the chaos of human lives engaged in surviving anew every day; at other times they were filled with hope at having witnessed a patient recovering from their deathbed. It was an emotional roller coaster. Petra focused on fundraising from international NGOs and churches. When Johan was not at the shacks, he was studying new research on HIV-AIDS. He trained young volunteers on caregiving, and treated ailments ranging from mouth sores to tuberculosis.

Petra wrote deeply personal and earnest letters to the donors. It was this approach that kept their work fully funded. She liked to use the story about saving millions of starfish, vomited up by the sea, one by one. She would say that she was aware that it was impossible to save all of them, but the ones they managed to throw back gave her the strength to wake up and do it again the next day. For her, it was enough that she made a difference to somebody's life. On difficult days, Johan felt his source of strength came from this incredible woman.

It was on one of these long, hard days that they arrived home to be confronted by a screaming baby wrapped in a blanket on their doorstep. They looked at each other with shock and disbelief. Petra picked up the screaming infant, placed it against her chest, and hushed it. Johan stood rooted in front of the door, trying to think of the next step. The baby quieted, and Petra became quiet along with her.

"You shall be with child," she said softly.

"What?" Johan asked.

"And the Lord said, 'You shall be with child.' Remember that story of Abraham and Sarah, they were old and well advanced in years. The Lord appeared to them and said—"

"Oh no no no, Petra, we can't. We are too old and too busy to raise a child. Please, tomorrow morning we're going to the police. We don't even know if this child is sick, or God knows what." Johan was panicking when he saw the look on her face. "Maybe the mother was drunk and she will come back sober tomorrow," he said. But he saw complete determination in Petra's eyes. She was going to fight him on this.

They used the fortified milk formula that they kept for the positive new moms who couldn't breastfeed. The baby suckled energetically like a thirsty new calf, and fell asleep contentedly. All of the dormant maternal instincts in Petra were unleashed. She was completely and utterly taken by this new miracle of life they had found. She didn't hear any of Johan's protests. In her excitement, she didn't even want to go to the police. If it had been in her power, she would have kept the baby without dealing with any of the legal red tape.

Johan managed to convince and pacify her by arguing that they could keep the baby only after reporting the matter to the police and applying for legal guardianship, should no one come to claim her. He did not think that social welfare would let them keep the baby.

The following day, the police came to the house to take a statement. They said, with authority, that legally the baby should be given to social welfare "until we get to the bottom of this." Everyone knew it would take ages to get to the bottom of anything.

Petra's voice was cracking as if she was about to cry. "All I'm saying is that we have a loving home right here and I can look after the child myself while you 'get to the bottom' of whatever it is you think you will find."

The police left and said they would come back with social welfare to take the baby. They seemed defeated by the lady's determination. She was fiercely protective of the baby. Johan couldn't stand to see Petra distressed and still had a particular dislike for the police. He asked the policeman if he had children, and the man said yes. "Well, Officer, we have never had children, even though we wanted to for a long time. So can you see what this is doing to my wife?"

The policeman was baffled by this couple fighting for a black baby. "Bloody bleeding heart liberals," he mumbled as he got into the car.

A curious neighbor called out, "Is everything all right there, Petra?"

Petra gushed out the whole story of the miracle found on her doorstep. "Can you tell me, what is the word for being found in isiZulu?"

"Tholakele, the word is Tholakele," said the neighbor, who was still in her pajamas, and was now standing in their yard cooing over the baby. "She is so adorable," she said.

Johan had lost the fight, and the idea of being a father was growing in him as well. They stood there cooing, filled with anxiety, anticipating the arrival of the social welfare people. Meanwhile the baby slept peacefully. "You have been found," Petra whispered to the baby, "and I shall name you Princess Tholakele." She looked back at Johan who was peering over her shoulder. He nodded, and it was sealed.

They drew strength from each other and geared themselves up for the fight of their lives with social welfare. The knock on their door sent cold shivers down their spines. They opened it, only to be relieved that it was Mbali, the social worker who served the same area of the shacks where they did their home visits. She was a sweet lady, with an unhurried, calm determination in her work with the children at the shacks.

Petra and Johan were comforted that she was handling their case. She told them that adoption would be a lengthy process that would start once the police had conducted a thorough investigation to find whoever had abandoned the baby. Meanwhile, they needed to convince social welfare to allow them to keep the child in their care. Their community involvement and Johan's medical background would stand them in good stead. Their age, both in their late fifties, and the fact that they were of a different race and cultural background to the child could be a problem, though. They hadn't thought about these things.

"Yes, the child is black," Petra argued, "but how do you determine her cultural background? She's probably not more than five days old. She could be Zulu, Xhosa, Congolese or anything. I would like them to tell me how they determine her cultural background!"

Mbali calmed her down, reminding her that she was on their side. "I'm in your corner. You know that I will do my best for you, but right now I'm advising you that if you want to fight to win, you'd better get yourself a good lawyer."

They realized that their lives had just changed in the blink of an eye. The harder things seemed to get, the more determined they were. After Mbali's visit, they went baby shopping for everything possible to make the life of their new miracle comfortable. Petra subscribed to baby magazines and found a support group for parents with cross-racially adopted babies.

Mbali had given them the number of a hotshot lawyer friend of hers who had just got back to town. She said the woman was someone who fought like a bull terrier, never letting go, especially in children's cases.

"She only takes cases that are important to her," Mbali explained. "She's a bit strange, but don't be put off. She'll fight for you until you get the legal right to be parents to this little princess." Petra held on to the piece of paper as though her life depended on it. "Her name is Nonceba Hlathi," Mbali said. And added as an afterthought, "It means bush."

Johan felt his skin prickle for a moment. But it would be just too much of a coincidence. He sat quietly and thoughtfully while Mbali and Petra talked through the red tape.

"And what are you thinking about so seriously, Princess's father?" Petra asked teasingly after Mbali had left.

All his memories of Zimkitha had come flooding back, and he had to steady himself to make the phone call to the lawyer.

The phone rang and rang, and then suddenly a voice came on the line. "Hi, this is Nonceba—"

"Hello, my—"

"...leave a message and I'll get back to you." A long beep followed her recorded voice.

Johan started again.

CHAPTER SEVENTEEN

"Where is the baby?" Cleanman asked when Mvelo returned empty-handed from hospital.

"It died," she lied without emotion.

Cleanman was dumbfounded. He was wondering just how much bad luck one young girl could have, first losing her mother and then her baby. After a long silence, he said, "It's probably for the best, young one."

She nodded in agreement.

She was too numb to cry and her mind was already on her next plan, to check if Sabekile was safe. The next day was rubbish collection day, when the shack dwellers were out in full force. She went to town as if to rummage through the bins, but only one house was her target. She kept a low profile, but was keenly observing if Sabekile was there. Her heart leaped when she saw them, the old white couple, with her baby. The woman was cradling the baby in her arms as the husband helped her into the passenger seat, and then went round to drive.

Mvelo waited near the house, and not long afterwards, they returned with the police. They were talking and showing the police where they had found the screaming baby. The police left, but soon after that, a lady in a dull suit and sensible shoes arrived at the house. Her car had the social welfare emblem on it. Mvelo wanted to scream because she thought it meant that her baby was going to be sent to one of those overcrowded institutions where other children and minders

abuse the younger ones. She was very relieved when she saw them come out talking amicably, and the social worker lady left without the baby. The smiling couple still had her baby with them. Her faith in her solemn prayer was restored.

Day in and day out, Mvelo continued to loiter around the house, keeping an eye on who was coming and going. She was careful not to be noticed, but she couldn't stay away; the pull was too powerful. She still had a strong, imprint-like feeling on her arm from cradling Sabekile when she was in the hospital, and she longed to feel the softness of her baby's skin again.

After about a month had passed, one day Mvelo saw the man of the house drive out and the woman, holding Sabekile, waving him goodbye and closing the front door. Mvelo became reckless. Beside herself, she went straight to the door and knocked.

The woman opened the door again with Sabekile. "Yes, young lady, how can I help you?" She had a practiced smile on her face, acting as though she didn't notice that Mvelo smelled like hot refuse and hadn't been in water for a week.

"Madam, I am hungry. Do you have anything for me to eat?" It was the only thing she could think of saying, and it was the truth, even though it wasn't the reason she was there.

"I think we must get you a change of clothes first and get you freshened up. You look like you're having a hard time," the woman said, the kindness never leaving her eyes, despite the offensive odor. She gave Mvelo a cake of soap and pointed her to an outside room that had a shower. "Go and get yourself cleaned up, and I'll bring you a change of clothes."

Perhaps it was the kindness of the woman and the scent of the Breeze soap, Mvelo's favorite, that reminded her of her mother, which brought rivers of tears to her eyes. Or perhaps it was the sight of her sore breasts, full of milk, with no child to suckle. But under that warm, soothing shower, she cried out all her tears.

When Petra walked in after a while, she found Mvelo on her knees, overcome by her private grief. She switched off the taps and wrapped Mvelo's body in a warm, soft towel, bringing back memories of when she was a child living in Sipho's house with her mother, before she knew anything of poverty.

"It will be all right," Petra said softly. "Come into the house and meet Princess Tholakele."

Inside there were pictures of the couple with her Sabekile. Mvelo changed into a jeans skirt and a red, cotton T-shirt with a Coca-Cola logo on the back. Petra looked her over and smiled. "What is your name?" she asked.

The question jolted Mvelo back to the present, and she said the first thing that passed through her mind. "My name is Dora," she lied. She was scared now because she felt she had come too close.

"Nice to meet you, Dora, my name is Petra. And this here," pointing to Mvelo's smiling Sabekile, "is my Princess Tholakele."

Mvelo stared at the baby, too dumbfounded to say anything. Her cheeks were full, she was dressed in a beautiful, pink jumpsuit, and she looked the picture of contentment. Mvelo thanked God for making sure that she was safe in the house of these kind strangers. Petra gave Mvelo a warm plate of *bobotie*. She hated raisins, but she gulped it down. She hadn't had a good square meal for some time.

While Mvelo ate, Petra told her that it was a big day for them because Johan, her husband, had gone to meet with a lawyer who was helping them legalize the adoption of Princess. Mvelo was relieved, and absorbed the warmth and the kindness of the house as she listened.

<hr />

When she stood up to leave, she touched Sabekile. She had to do it. It was a pull as strong as a physical ache. All the while that she was there, she had been fighting herself from grabbing the baby and greedily holding on to her. Instead, now she simply touched her small hand, trying hard to make it look casual. The baby grabbed her hand firmly with both of her own and tried to put it into her mouth. The lady laughed, and said everything went into Princess's mouth these days. Mvelo thanked Petra for her kindness and said she would be on her way.

As she was leaving, Petra told Mvelo about the work she did with her husband, and gave her a plastic bag full of clothes. She said she could see that Mvelo had fallen on hard times. It was the first time anyone had ever asked Mvelo not to be offended for being given handouts. It was the strangest feeling. She felt warm inside, not like the dirty, smelly beggar that she was when she had arrived at the house. The lump in her throat returned.

She couldn't verbalize a thank you, she simply nodded and her eyes clouded with tears. Petra squeezed her shoulder and repeated that it would be all right.

Mvelo cried for most of that night and the next day. It wasn't a sad cry, but a cry from fullness that she felt in her stomach and her chest. It had been a strange day.

The singing from the tent filtered into Mvelo's ears like a dream. It was from the other side of the hill and the wind carried the voices to her side of the shacks. She woke up with a start, and her heart was thumping like a drum. She ran to Cleanman's shack, just to be sure that she wasn't hearing voices. "Cleanman, can you hear that noise?" she asked him.

"Young one, you surprise me," he said. "How can you say the preaching of the gospel is noise? You and your mother regularly attended the revivals of Pastor Nhlengethwa."

Mvelo froze. Cleanman looked at her quizzically. He had mentioned his name and resurrected him again. How could he do that? Mvelo had killed him in her mind. Now he was back.

The music quieted and she walked back to her shack. Her head felt heavy, as if she had flu. Her mouth tasted metallic. She drank a glass of water and tried to wash the taste way. "You are all children of God," the voice came on the wind again. The sound of it weakened her muscles. The only glass she had fell from her hand and smashed into pieces on the floor. Her bladder loosened, warming her thighs. She began to sweat and it felt like the shack was closing in on her.

"I ask the men in this tent to stand up and say, 'I will be my sister's keeper.'" The voice was gaining righteous fervor. Barely nine months after tearing apart Mvelo's world, Nhlengethwa was back, scouting for more victims.

She trembled and cried out from the hot anger she felt inside.

"Be men who can be counted on," the voice came again. "You were born to be protectors, my brothers. Come to God and give your pledge to protect His angels. Remember what He said, 'Let the children come unto me.'" His fervor was reaching fever pitch, leaving Mvelo with no doubt that the lion had spotted his next prey.

His sermon convinced Mvelo that she needed to do something. He had to be stopped.

The following night, she walked the long way to the other side of the hill. She waited and watched as the tent filled up with people. The music began, and there he was, her violator. Mvelo's curses hadn't done anything to him. He stood there on the podium, tall and strong, well fed by the money of those desperate for salvation. The sight of him made her feel small and unsure of what to do next.

It was when he began to preach that she remembered her mother's funeral; how women started a song each time they wanted to discourage a eulogy that was inappropriate. "*Amahlathi, amahlathi aphelile. Akusekho ukucasha*. The forest is done, there is nowhere to hide," Mvelo began to sing with a conviction she didn't feel. From the dark of the tent he couldn't see her, but the spotlight was on him so she could see him. The congregation joined with her song.

Mvelo walked slowly into the light. The elders eyed her with uncertainty; they didn't know what to do, so she walked freely to the front without being stopped.

By this time, she could see the recognition in his eyes.

She took off her dress and her panties and stood in front of him and the congregation, naked as the day she was born.

Before anyone could do anything, Nhlengethwa fell like a log. His shocked, ugly heart had failed. The men ran to his side and the women threw a blanket to Mvelo, which she took and covered herself.

No one got close to her. Even in church, the fears of witchcraft were strong. Some threw salt, which they kept nearby, towards her, and others called the name of Jesus to remove the evil spirits in her. She simply wrapped the blanket around her, picked up her dress and panties, and walked out into a beautiful, balmy Durban night.

She walked towards the sea, and when she reached the beach, she sat and listened to the waves whispering their secrets to her.

CHAPTER EIGHTEEN

The news of Sipho's death finally reached Nonceba. It was not long after Zola died. The many voices that usually disturbed her were quieting down; being back on the continent of her birth connected her again, and the troubling dreams began lessening too.

In her preoccupation with healing herself, she had to completely shut down thoughts of others to concentrate on finding her center again, which had become lost along the way. She hadn't lost hope of finding her father, but she no longer obsessed about it. She had stopped looking actively, after she consulted with a charlatan of a seer who said that the only way he could connect with the spirit of her father was by sleeping with her. She spat in his face and left without a word.

Eventually all roads led back to Durban, the place where she had found love with Sipho, and her motherly instinct through caring for Mvelo.

Her thoughts of Mvelo pricked her like a thorn. She felt guilty about breaking her promise to Mvelo, but a part of her knew that it had to be done. To separate from Sipho, she'd had to let go of everything connected to him.

Part of her reason for coming back to Durban was that she wanted to do a course in homeopathy at the Durban University of Technology. Finally she began to visit her old haunts again, and was shocked and heartbroken when she arrived at her old legal firm downtown and heard about Sipho.

Johan's message on her voicemail drew her back into legal work, even though she had hoped not to go back to the law. Something about the case pulled her in. He spoke of their legal battle with social welfare, who were threatening to take the child away, and she thought of her grandmother who was brought up in an orphanage before she was adopted.

"Yes, Mbali told me. I'm glad that you're dealing with her," she said when she returned his call. "If she trusts you, as you say she does, she'll buy us some time while I take a few weeks to settle in. I'm sure my former colleagues will accommodate me, and we'll fight this together." She was trying to convince herself as much as to convince him.

She felt the old rush coming back to her. The excitement of a good legal fight coming her way left her feeling flushed. She was back, working with people who really needed her help.

As she sat on the futon in the beachfront flat she had rented, she went through the notes she had been taking while talking to Johan. What a sad story of desperation, leaving a child on the doorstep of strangers. She wondered about the mother who had abandoned the child. It left her feeling sad.

Three weeks after Johan's call, she managed to convince Sipho's former partners to take her back to deal with pro bono cases and start a legal clinic as part of their social responsibility program. When Johan called again as arranged, she was in high spirits, because she was going back on her own terms.

Johan agreed to meet her mid-morning at Tribeca on Florida Road.

CHAPTER NINETEEN

Despite his better judgment, after Mbali had mentioned Nonceba's name, Johan had allowed himself a tiny seed of hope. Perhaps this woman could be related to Zimkitha and she could help them find his daughter. He set up the meeting with her, and then he became a bundle of nerves. Petra couldn't understand it, and he felt he had to finally come clean with her and tell her what he thought.

"Why didn't you tell me!" she said, appearing excited.

"I didn't want to get our hopes up, in case nothing came of it," he said simply.

"Well, we will soon know one way or the other, so you had better get there and find out. We need this woman to help us with Princess."

As he was picking up his keys and heading for the car, he had to turn around and dash to the bathroom, where he heaved out the contents of his stomach.

Petra silently handed him a towel and stared at him for a minute. Then she said, "I'll do it. I will go and meet her, and I'll tell her you had a case of the jitters about the adoption."

"Would you?" He looked at her gratefully. "I am sorry, Petra. I thought I was ready but now I just can't."

"The other thing we could do," said Petra, always the practical one, "is that we could all go, and you could sit somewhere else and join us later, if you feel up to it."

They were early. He sat opposite the table that Petra chose, and ordered some tea to calm his nerves.

Nonceba arrived in her red Golf. As she crossed the street, in her jeans and cotton top, she was the image of Zimkitha all those years ago. Johan jolted and burned his tongue on his tea. There was no doubt in his mind that the woman with the big afro, walking towards the restaurant, was Zimkitha's daughter. His hands began to shake. It was all too much, so he stood up, left some money for the tea, and hurried out.

Petra looked at her husband and she knew. She stood up and waved Nonceba over to her table.

Nonceba saw Petra with Princess Tholakele, and walked over to them. "Mrs. Steyn?" she said, extending her hand. "I thought I was meeting with your husband."

"He woke up with an upset stomach this morning," she said, "and we didn't want to cancel, so I thought that I should come over with Princess to meet you." All the while she was taking in the facial features in front of her. She had Johan's forehead, the slight curl in her lips, and a distinct dimple in her chin. When Petra turned to take a casual look at Johan's table, he was nowhere to be seen.

"So, Mrs. Steyn, it seems we are in for a tough fight." Nonceba was gearing herself up and playing with the chubby cheeks of the baby.

Petra had to camouflage the shock she felt at seeing her husband's daughter looking back at her. As their conversation progressed, she began to relax, and they focused on the baby and the case. They parted with a promise to fight to the end for Princess Tholakele.

When Petra got home, she filled Johan in on the meeting. She also confirmed to him that there was no doubt in her mind that Nonceba was his daughter. She understood his predicament, but she also knew that something had to be done. "What if we keep quiet about what we know until after the case is concluded?" she suggested. They agreed that it would probably be the best way to proceed.

After the meeting with Petra was concluded, Nonceba headed for the shacks. Spending time with the baby made her think of her own maternal responsibilities, and she had started to feel increasingly guilty about abandoning Mvelo. She had to look for her and find out how she was doing.

Mvelo had managed to dodge most of the visitors who had tried to come to her shack after the birth of her baby, and now she was distracted by the death of Reverend Nhlengethwa. A part of her felt uneasy; it wasn't her intention for him to die like that. She wanted to tell her side of the story to the congregation, to expose his hypocrisy and lies. She was angry that she didn't have a chance to do that. As far as the congregation was concerned, he had died a saint. She wasn't sad that he had died, but she did wonder if she was evil, as the congregants were saying.

A knock on the door stopped the train of thoughts railing in her brain. "Who is it?" she asked. She had learned never to open the door to just anyone. It was a weak, rickety door that would give in with one kick, but as long as it was closed, she felt OK. There was no answer, so she stayed put, but the knocking continued.

Cleanman was observing from his shack, and he made his way down.

Mvelo heard him speaking to someone in harsh tones, and then he said: "Young one, you better open up for this one." He had a vague idea of who Nonceba was; Zola had made it known that Nonceba had stolen Sipho from her.

Mvelo slowly opened the door, and there she was.

This picture of health in front of her made Mvelo angry. She closed the door and told her to fuck off back to America, screaming that nobody needed her stupid packages here. "You can keep your Dr. Peppers and Mars bars," she shouted, tears welling up in her eyes.

"Young one, please, that is not a way to speak to old people. Your mother taught you better than that."

"Cleanman, stay out of this. You can also fuck off to your shack, and stop acting like my father." She was sobbing now, feeling raw all over again.

There was silence outside the door. She peeped through a crack and saw both of them walking away toward Cleanman's shack. Watching them walk away like that made her feel helpless. She had her mother's pride; she wanted them to beg her to open the door. She sat on the floor and cried, while they sat in front of Cleanman's door, waiting for her to open.

"Where is her mother?" Nonceba asked Cleanman, who hesitated and gave sketchy details of what had happened, saying that it wasn't his place to tell her.

"It is best that you wait for her to calm down and she will tell you everything." Cleanman had no illusions about his role in Mvelo's life. She was a girl who needed looking after, but she was also capable of handling herself. It was one of the things Mvelo liked about him.

After a while the conversation dried up between Nonceba and Cleanman, and she stood up and said, "This is ridiculous. I am going to speak to her, even if I have to kick the door down." She warned Mvelo to move out of the way because she was entering her shack, come hell or high water. Then she pushed the door with all her weight behind her until it opened.

Mvelo could not look her in the eye because she was so angry. Nonceba was someone real to blame for all her misfortunes. She began to shake. All the anger of being alone finally rose to the surface. Then she felt relief, she was no longer alone. But the child in her still wanted to pout and sulk.

Nonceba stood there, taking in all the desperation she met

in the shack. She knelt and collected Mvelo into her arms and held her until she couldn't cry any longer. She whispered soothingly, like a prayer, in a language Mvelo could not understand.

Life had been hard on Mvelo, she had learned to be deeply distrustful of people, and she was afraid to trust Nonceba now. It was only because she was asleep that Nonceba was able to transport her to her flat without a fight. She fell asleep on Nonceba's lap, and Cleanman carried her to the car, relieved there was finally someone capable to look after her.

She woke up in the flat with Nonceba standing sadly by the bed. Nonceba said that maDlamini had told her everything about her pregnancy and the loss of the baby.

"Well, who is the father? Is that why you quit school?" Nonceba wanted to know.

Mvelo didn't answer. They were eating fish and chips, her favorite meal. Nonceba had remembered, Mvelo noted as she tucked in, forgetting all about her pride.

Nonceba took a different tack. "You can tell me anything you want, you know that, right?"

Mvelo simply looked down at her food and continued eating.

"You must have been through hell. I heard about your mother and Sipho. I'm so grateful I found you. You can stay here with me now."

"I don't want to stay here, I need to get back to my shack." Mvelo stopped eating and became very agitated.

"But Mvelo, you're too young to be living alone," Nonceba tried to reason with her.

"Well you can't make me stay here. You can't put me through what I had to deal with when my mother got sick. You have to find someone else to look after you. I can't do it again, I can't." She was beside herself.

"But what are you talking about? I'm not sick, and I'm not asking you to look after me. I want to look after you. You need someone to look after you for a change." Nonceba held her hand until she calmed down.

"You are not sick?" Mvelo asked hesitantly.

Nonceba smiled. "No, I'm not sick."

"But Sipho made my mother sick, and another woman in his office," she said, crying fresh tears.

"Oh, no no no, gal, I'm not sick. We can go to the doctor for tests and you'll see that I'm not sick. But now it's late. We'd better get some sleep and we'll make that decision tomorrow."

Mvelo looked at her long and hard. A healthy-looking woman stared back at her. Mvelo had looked up to her once, and she wanted to trust her again, but she couldn't, not yet. She would only believe her after seeing the results.

All she knew for certain was that she was never going to look after another sick person again.

They went to a New Start clinic where Nonceba took the test in front of a vigilant Mvelo, and was given a clean bill of health. Mvelo seemed more relieved than Nonceba was, but Nonceba had had no fears, she had always been uncompromising about using a condom.

Mvelo decided there and then to tell Nonceba about being raped, and that Sabekile hadn't died, that she'd left the baby with a family who could take care of her. Nonceba listened quietly, and by the end of the story, she looked dazed, her face as hard as a statue. "It's my fault," she said. "I was self-absorbed and selfish after I broke things off with Sipho. I neglected you and the promises I made to you. I am so sorry." Her voice was constricted with pain.

The concrete walls that Mvelo had surrounded herself

with crumbled, the floodgates opened, and she sobbed for
what felt like hours.

She was awoken by Nonceba the next morning. "Come,"
she said, and she drove north of Durban until they reached
Westbrook Beach, where she rented a speedboat.

The man looked at them strangely, bemused that two black
women were renting a boat.

"Are you going to rent us the boat or not, we don't have all
day." Nonceba's edge was back.

He gave them what they wanted and made them sign an
indemnity form, clearing him of any liability should anything
happen to them. They changed into the wetsuits that came
with the boat, and Nonceba instructed Mvelo to hold on
tight and off they went into the sea. Once they were out far
enough, where the waves were gentle, Nonceba switched
off the noisy boat and let it bob about. Everything around
them was absolutely quiet. Even the silence between them
was welcome.

After some time, Nonceba said, "This is what it should be
like. Nature intended for us to be peaceful and safe."

"Right," she said after a few more minutes had passed,
"you and I need to get rid of all this ugliness we're holding
onto inside of us, and this is the perfect place to do it. No one
will hear us or disturb us. I am so angry and so sad for what
happened to you that I don't have words. And I know that if
I don't do anything about it, it will surely kill me. And if I'm
feeling this way, I'm sure you must have developed a rock
for a heart too, and you're too young for that. So I think we
should just scream."

Mvelo was taken aback at first, but she remembered the
old Nonceba and her crazy ways that had helped her so much
when she was young and feeling insecure, so she decided

to trust her. She was tentative at first, but seeing Nonceba letting go like that helped to rid her of her inhibitions, and she screamed until she had no voice left. They molested the peace on the open ocean.

Then she began to laugh. She laughed and laughed uncontrollably, until she sank to the bottom of the boat and wept until she had no tears left, and a strange peace descended on her.

They landed back on shore later in the afternoon in one piece. The obnoxious man was happy to get his boat back and see the backs of them "cheeky cheeks," as he called them. Nonceba was feeling too good to argue with him.

On the drive back to Durban, Nonceba asked Mvelo, "What of the baby, do you know anything about her since you left her?"

"Yes," Mvelo said, "I visited the family pretending to be begging. The woman in the house let me in and fed me." Mvelo didn't like where this conversation was going. She thought of the police. She could be arrested and sent to a juvenile institution.

"We should report the matter to the police," Nonceba said, "and I could offer to adopt you and the baby. After all you're like family to me. In fact, you're the only family I have now," she said sadly.

"What if I get arrested? Please, let's not do it like that. I'm ashamed of what I did and Sabekile is fine where she is. That woman told me that they were fighting to keep her with them," Mvelo pleaded.

"Wait a minute, do you know the name of the woman who took in your child?" Nonceba asked.

"Yes," Mvelo said, puzzled by the question, and trying to remember the name. "I think it was Peta, or Patricia, something like that."

"Not Petra?" Nonceba was getting excited.

"Yes, I think that's it, Petra," Mvelo said.

Nonceba smiled. She had a phone call to make.

CHAPTER TWENTY

It was Johan who answered the phone.

"Hello, Mr. Steyn, this is Nonceba. There have been some developments in your case and I think we should meet as soon as possible. It's not something I can discuss on the phone. Can we make it at the same place where I met your wife, sometime tomorrow morning?"

Johan felt his stomach turn.

"What it is? You look worried," Petra said when he got off the phone.

"I don't know. Nonceba wants to meet us. She says there are new developments in the case." Since the arrival of this baby, it seemed their lives had been turned upside down, and it was draining him, reminding him of past mistakes that he would rather forget.

"I can meet her alone again if you are not ready," Petra offered.

"You know, Petra, I can't run away forever. At some point, I have got to face her. If we wait until after the case, it will be another deception, which may make her even angrier. I will come with you, and if I feel strong enough, I will tell her who I am."

The following morning they all got into the car—Johan, Petra, and baby Princess.

On the other side of town in Morningside, where they had moved from the beachfront flat to a cottage with enough space for the two of them, Nonceba had to work hard to

convince Mvelo to meet these people and see if they were
the ones who had her baby. "I could be wrong, but if I'm not
we can fight for Sabekile," she said.

The only thing that made Mvelo happy was that Nonceba
agreed to hold off reporting it to the police. So they got ready
and walked to Tribeca from the cottage.

"It's her, the woman, it's her," Mvelo said as they
approached, holding Nonceba's hand tightly. "Please let's go
back, she'll recognize me," she said, pulling Nonceba away.

"But Mvelo, don't you see. This is good. You'll get your baby
back and we can be a family. Don't you want that?"

Mvelo did. She wanted it so badly, but she couldn't face the
woman and tell her that she was taking the baby back. She
had been so kind to her, and now she was about to break her
heart. It was too late to turn back, though, they had already
seen them coming.

Petra looked confused. "I know you. You came to my house
the other day," she said, as Nonceba and Mvelo sat down.

Mvelo's stomach went cold and turned somersaults.

Nonceba explained about Sipho and her connection to
Mvelo. When she got to the part about Mvelo abandoning
her baby, Petra couldn't hold back her tears. "I knew it,"
she said. "I could see you were the mother. What now? How
are we going to deal with this?" She was holding Princess
Tholakele tightly.

Johan sat quietly, numb as a stone. He avoided looking
at Petra because her tears were cutting into him. Mvelo
couldn't look at anyone at the table. She was too ashamed
about her part in the mess.

An uncomfortable silence fell all around as it became clear
that Nonceba and Mvelo wanted to take the baby from them.

Finally Johan couldn't stand it any more. He felt he was
being punished for his sins, but Petra didn't deserve this.

◁────◇────▷

"I used to know a lady by the name of Zimkitha Hlathi," he blurted out. "She was thrown in jail for kissing me in public, but by then it was too late because she was already carrying my child." He talked quickly before he lost his nerve.

There was stunned silence all round.

Johan reached into his jacket pocket and took out a picture of a woman who was the image of Nonceba, just a little darker with slightly tighter curls. Nonceba couldn't remember her mother in person, but she had seen pictures of her. The one Johan held was of her mother all right. Nonceba looked at the picture, looked at her father, and burst into tears.

Petra stood up with Princess and asked Mvelo to join her to give Johan and Nonceba some privacy. Mvelo was too dumbfounded to say anything, and followed Petra to another table. They sat there, too scared to say anything to each other.

Petra was cradling Princess and fussing over her and, as she watched, Mvelo made up her mind. She had given Sabekile up. She had prayed for her baby to find a good home, and she had. If this woman would allow her to be a part of her baby's life, to see her whenever she wanted, she would let her adopt Sabekile.

As much as she was happy to have Nonceba back, Nonceba had left her before. What would stop her from doing it again? And what would she do then? How would she look after Sabekile? She did not want her daughter to face a day of hunger.

"She belongs with you," Mvelo said to Petra. "If you allow me to visit her, she can stay with you."

Petra wept, and Mvelo took the baby from her arms and held her. She drank in the warm, soft feeling and her milky smell. She felt immense love for her child.

◄————◇————►

Waiters at the restaurant looked puzzled at the obvious drama unfolding before them. Johan was rooted in his seat, too scared to move.

"I had given up. I looked and looked, and then eventually I gave up," said Nonceba between gulps of emotions. She stretched her hands across the table and reached for Johan's. It was more than he had hoped for.

"She was the most beautiful woman I had ever seen," he said. "I loved her but I was a coward."

Nonceba looked down at the picture. "Tell me about her," she said. "I want to hear it from you. My grandmother told me what she knew, but she didn't know much about her life in Hillbrow."

It was around 6 p.m. when they finally left Tribeca, all of them thoroughly exhausted. They had still not discussed any of the details regarding the adoption, so they planned another meeting in Manor Gardens at Petra and Johan's house.

Johan was relieved that Nonceba had not rejected him. Zimkitha's burning eyes were replaced with the loving eyes of Nonceba. She concluded that she had been brought back to Durban to complete her search.

Johan and Petra couldn't believe their many blessings. First they had found a baby looking for their care, then a daughter they had searched for high and low, and a teenager who had chosen their home for her baby to belong to.

When Mvelo told Nonceba of her decision to let Petra and Johan keep the baby, Nonceba reminded her that they still had to face the court.

Mvelo fell asleep with her head buzzing.

◄——◇——►

CHAPTER TWENTY-ONE

The tension in the court was palpable after the rumor went around that an underage mother had admitted to abandoning her baby at the Steyns' house. Cleanman was there, and many others from the shacks had come to support the kind doctor and his wife who had nursed many of them back to health. Some had threatened to protest should the state decide to take the baby away. "*Sizobhosha la enkantolo. We will shit right here in court*," they shouted their threats outside the doors. Inside the court, the magistrate had to use her gavel a few times to call for order to calm the excited murmurings.

Petra, Johan, and Princess Sabekile were at the front with Nonceba and Cleanman—all the people that Mvelo considered her family. The shack-dwellers stood behind them throughout the case. Mvelo was grateful for the network of love and support that seemed to extend before her eyes.

After much to-ing and fro-ing, it became clear that the state's lawyers did not have much ground to stand on; Mvelo had no means to take care of the child. She insisted that she fully comprehended what she was saying when she stated that the Steyns were the preferred adoptive parents for her daughter. The fact that she had risked getting caught by monitoring their house counted in her favor as evidence that she wasn't a heartless animal who had abandoned her baby.

When Nonceba was questioned about her self-appointed guardianship of Mvelo, she stated that she had been Sipho's common-law wife and was therefore effectively her stepmother. Mvelo sat and watched the proceedings from a screen in camera. Her nervousness turned into excitement as Nonceba appeared to be gaining more ground. It took a few appearances before the judgment was finally made, and the Steyns were declared Sabekile's adoptive parents.

Mvelo agreed to go back to school the following year and repeat Grade 8. Nonceba insisted that she should return to the same school, and confront the rumors of her abandoning her child. It was the only way, she said, that Mvelo would be able to regain her confidence and not feel ashamed of what had happened.

When the school year began, Mvelo wondered how she would cope. Even though she was only turning sixteen, she felt so much older now. And she wasn't prepared for the stares and meaningful glances that she got, particularly from the teachers. Her old friends were in higher grades now. But she told herself that she would simply work hard.

After school she spent most of her time in Manor Gardens. Sabekile's first word was Mama, and she said it to Mvelo, who nearly fainted with excitement. She looked at Petra, who nodded at her, smiling. Mvelo squeezed Sabekile's little body so tight that the baby squirmed under her weight.

While they were playing with Sabekile one evening, Petra said to Mvelo, "You know, I knew the first day you came here that you were her mother. But now, as she grows, there's no doubt that she's yours."

Mvelo thought the baby looked like her mother, and she felt a stab of sadness that Zola would never get to meet her.

CHAPTER TWENTY-TWO

Nonceba had a wide circle of friends, and she liked entertaining at home. Mvelo usually felt a bit out of place at these gatherings; that is, until she developed her first serious crush. He was in his mid-twenties, and she was just twenty, doing her matric, but he made her feel that she was a woman, not a schoolgirl.

"Sisi Nonceba, you never told me that you have such a beautiful sister," he said, charming Mvelo, taking her hand and kissing it. The sensation of his lips on her hand caught her by surprise, and she thanked God for her dark skin at this moment, so he couldn't see her blush.

"What's your name, beautiful?" he asked, looking at her with his big smiling eyes.

"Mvelo," she said, watching him closely, trying to gauge his game.

"A perfect name for a perfect lady," he said, and she smiled shyly. "It's a pleasure to meet you. My name is Cetshwayo Jama kaZulu," he said proudly. "I worked with your sister when I was an intern. She's a real taskmaster, but we do love her."

Nonceba watched this spectacle with amusement. She didn't correct him about them not being sisters. Mvelo was glad about that.

While others at the party discussed weighty issues such as democracy, Cetshwayo sat by Mvelo's side and asked her about her plans after she finished school. No man had ever shown an interest in her like this, in what she thought and wanted to do with her life, and she found herself talking easily to him.

"I would like to make a career in music," she said, voicing her dream for the first time.

He spoke about his love of the law and how much still needed to change. Mvelo thought how, if it hadn't been for lawyers, she could have lost Sabekile. She was inspired by his passion.

They began dating, with permission from Nonceba, of course, and he opened Mvelo up to a whole new world: university talks about the African Renaissance, poetry festivals and readings. Some of it went over her head, but that didn't matter, they were things she enjoyed doing with Cetshwayo. Some of the performances simply made her feel, she didn't need to understand them, she felt them in her veins.

One evening Cetshwayo stood up and read. The words were so beautiful. Mvelo began to sing a soft melody along with him. He looked surprised, but smiled and continued reading. They were in perfect harmony.

On the way home they were silent, understanding that something had changed. When he dropped her off, he kissed her on her cheek. It was their second kiss.

Only after she had written her exams and passed matric, he told her he knew about what she had been through. Nonceba had called him aside and threatened to cut off his manhood if he ever did anything to hurt Mvelo. "I knew you would do well," he said. And then he kissed her again, this time on the lips.

Sabekile was now a toddler and remained a great source of joy to Mvelo. She loved singing, in her own strange mix of Zulu, English, Afrikaans and Xhosa, and demanded that Mvelo sing to her too. One rainy Durban summer's day, she ran outside with her little arms spread and said, "Look, Mama, God's kisses." It brought a lump to Mvelo's throat, as it made her think of her mother. It was the kind of thing Zola would have said. She joined Sabekile with her arms outstretched, twirling in the rain.

After she passed matric, Mvelo registered at the University of KwaZulu-Natal to study journalism. Though she hoped to follow her dream of singing professionally, Nonceba had persuaded her to also study something practical, so that she would always be able to support herself. When they got home from registration, Nonceba launched into one of her long speeches about how proud she was of Mvelo. She hugged her, and didn't let her go for a long time, until Mvelo felt Nonceba's body begin to shake.

Mvelo stiffened and pulled away, and then she saw that Nonceba was crying. She was confused. "What is it?" she asked.

"Well, I have some news that I don't think you'll be happy about. I'm going back to the U.S. to do some studies on one of the Native American reservations. I'll be gone for three months, but I promise that I'll be back."

Mvelo could see that Nonceba was afraid she was not going to take it well, but she had a family now. She knew she would not be alone.

She and Cetshwayo drove Nonceba to the airport and saw her off on her journey. "She is something else, that one," Cetshwayo said as they waved her goodbye.

"That she is," Mvelo said, finally realizing that Nonceba was feeling the pull of her other ancestors too.

"So when do I get to introduce you to my mother?" Cetshwayo asked, out of the blue.

Mvelo had moved from infatuation to a quiet, comfortable kind of love. They had shared furnace kisses, but when it began to go further, she always froze. The ghost of Nhlengethwa hung over them. Cetshwayo always stopped her from apologizing. "It's not your fault, I know, it's that bastard who took advantage of you," he would try to reassure her, feeling frustrated, but with no one to vent to.

"Well," Mvelo said, "before we count our chickens, perhaps meeting your mother should be after a trip to a New Start clinic."

Mvelo had grown very wise in her twenty years, and she knew that whatever happened, she would have the strength to deal with it.

THE LOVABLE LOTHARIO AND THE SHACK LIVES

Afterword
by Futhi Ntshingila

We Kiss Them With Rain was inspired by many things but two incidents stand out for me.

One happened years ago when my aunt's lover passed away. He was a flashy taxi owner, a self-made man who loved women as if they were his religion. His house was always full of boys hanging out with him and hanging on to his every lecherous word. Unlike most characters who are self-made business people, he wasn't ruthless. He was likeable, funny, and very generous with his money. With the advent of HIV-AIDS in the 1990's, he got ill. Soon, he became a feature in a long blue gown on the side wall of his house, soaking in the sun and just hanging out with the boys who continued to visit and care for him.

In a bid to keep normalcy going, they would still make him laugh with lewd jokes even though the laughs were unnaturally louder and hollow, hiding the fear of what was to come. A few days before he passed away, he was weak but still laughing with the boys. He told the boys that at his funeral, he wanted all the females who came to the service not to wear underwear. He said he wanted this because he would be lying down and when they lined past to view his body, he would be smiling like a cat that got all the cream because his eyes would be feasting on what was under their dresses and skirts. The boys laughed but he cried and insisted they promise him to at least announce his wish.

Well, that was the talk of the township and a cause for many guffaws. Of course women didn't do it but it remained in my mind. Years later, I thought, *What if women did it? What if they agreed to do it?* So I sat down and wrote an unreal story of a man who was so loved by his women that, even after infecting them with HIV, they still worshipped the ground he walked on. They indulged him even in his death by stripping off their undies. I don't know what it all means to feminists, conservatives, moralists or whoever else but I know that when I wrote his story, I learned and felt something about love that is unconditional but dangerous too. I felt, at least in my imagination, a kind of surrender which I see some women do. The way women love men who can endanger them is something that normally gets me angry but with this experiment of mine in writing, I came close to seeing their perspective of being smothered to death by love laced with poison.

The second incident that inspired this story was about a decade ago when I worked as a reporter for a newspaper in Durban where, in summer, there can be fearsome flash floods. While rain may be a source of joy for farmers and innocent children to jump around and dance in it, for those living in shacks, it spells death and destruction.

After the rains, I went there in search of a story and a by line. I found women cleaning up and salvaging bits they could, while men were drinking their worries away. One family's grandmother and grandson were washed off by flash floods and their bodies found five kilometers away under a bridge.

Music was blaring from the *shebeens*, taxis were zigzagging through the streets and collecting people to go to town, a group of Indian neighbours were dishing out *biriyani*. I stood there looking and not knowing where to start. Two people had just died; shacks were knee deep in slushy mud; but people there were determined to keep the normalcy going. Of course, the dead would be buried, shacks would be cleaned out, and life will be lived. I can't remember what kind of article I wrote but I just knew that people like that—with lives and circumstances lived on the margins of society—should be known.

Q&A
with Futhi Ntshingila

1. **You've stated in the past that you see your work as "converting oral stories into a written form." How do oral stories inform your writing?**

   In the Zulu tradition, we are steeped in a rich history of oral tradition. Oral traditions in the continent were marginalized by the hegemonic processes of colonization. But in the margins, oral tradition continues to impact African lives and identities. My surname has seven sub-names; and in those sub-names lies the history of where my people came from, the characters of my people, including their tempers and funny anecdotes. Then we have folktales of fiction mixed with facts. Squatter camps are full of stories about people that are not written down. This is where I feel I come in—mixing facts and fiction to tell the stories of those whose stories would otherwise never be told.

2. **Both of your two novels are about women who learn to empower themselves in particularly disempowering circumstances. Can you talk about why this is an important theme to your work?**

   Ever since I can remember, I have been surrounded by women, starting with my mother and my three sisters, five aunties, and countless cousins, friends, and church ladies. My dad was the only male figure around really. We lived in the margins of society during the years of racial discrimination. Socio-economic environments were not in our favor. Men went to work in the mines and cities far from home and women had to make do mostly working in kitchens for white people. I don't remember hearing complaints but scant food was produced and stretched to fill our tummies and lives were lived. My writing is a way of honoring them for the many sacrifices they had to make.

3. **Can you tell us more about the situation in South Africa that leads to squatter towns? How are women and children particularly vulnerable in these squatter camps?**

During the apartheid government, black South Africans were moved miles away from the cities. There was a policy that demanded black people to have a special permission to live and work in the city. Democracy allowed for free movement which led to people putting up shacks to live and have easy access to the city to make a living. The structures of these shacks are not very strong.

During the height of apartheid, when men were separated from their families due to the work situation, strong family structures got blurred, which led to many young single mothers heading households. They become easy targets for men who either enter the home as boyfriends but in the end break the trust by molesting young girls. Sometimes it is rape attacks and grooming that leaves women and children as targets. There was a period where it was believed that sleeping with a virgin could cure HIV-AIDS.

4. **Can you tell us about the HIV–AIDS situation in South Africa?**

In the 1990's, HIV–AIDS became rampant in South Africa, claiming the lives of young people. Men in mines used sex-workers and infected wives in the villages. Young girls who slept with sugar daddies infected boyfriends and boyfriends who had more than one girlfriend infected more. Rapes of virgins by misled men who believed sleeping with a virgin could cure AIDS led to more lives ruined. It became a crisis.

With awareness campaigns and treatment, it has become a manageable disease now but it hasn't stopped affecting people's lives. The poor, young girls who fall in the claws of infected older men still face infections.

5. **Though Mvelo's situation seems hopeless, she ends up in the best possible circumstance by the end of the book, almost a fairy tale ending. Can you talk about your choice to give her a hopeful ending rather than what many would consider a more "realistic" ending?**

The story is grim and it is realistic. The ending is hopeful and it is realistic too. Not everyone comes out of the cycle of poverty but, with determination, people do make something of their lives.

Fortunately, I do not follow literary formats when I tell stories. I wouldn't have written this book if it had a grim ending. It would have been pointless for me. I think the ending is a fairy tale only if one believes every person who starts out poor ends up poor. I see this ending as a reality for many South Africans who are a growing middle class today. They claw their ways out of poverty, contrary to some people's belief that most black middle class people today are successful through corruption. No, many school mates who struggled with poverty like I did succeeded by working. They worked hard and knocked on doors, sometimes literally walking from door to door. I know it of my personal experience. Hard work and luck met up and made my life and the lives of many others a reality that can be perceived as hopeful.

Discussion Questions

1. In what ways is *We Kiss Them With Rain* a classic coming-of-age story and in what ways is it different?

2. What does this story suggest life is like for a young poor black woman growing up in South Africa? List the things that surprised you and list the things that didn't.

3. The back cover suggests that *We Kiss Them With Rain* uses elements of Shakespearean comedy to tell this tale. What does that mean? In what ways does this story remind you of classic Shakespearean comedies like *A Midsummer's Night's Dream*? In what ways is it different?

4. Futhi Ntshingila's use of the supernatural is subtle in *We Kiss Them With Rain*. Where do the supernatural elements of the story occur? Is the supernatural a symbol of power? Why or why not and how?

5. Would you consider this novel a feminist text? Why or why not?

6. At her mother's funeral, Mvelo reads her mother's favorite biblical verse about love. (*If I speak with the languages of men and of angels, but have not love, I am nothing, etc.*) How does this particular verse, and its meaning, intertwine with the characters' fates during the course of the novel? What is the role of "love" in this book?

7. What are the sexual politics of this book? How is

Nonceba's sexuality displayed differently than Zola's or Mvelo's? What is the history and culture behind those differences? From this book, what would you guess sex education (whether that occurs in families or institutions) in South Africa looks like? How might it be different in North America?

8. Consider the relationship between Sipho and Julia, his mother's employer. What are the power and gender dynamics at play in that relationship?

9. Both Johan and Zimkitha seemed to be with each other as an act of defiance. Was any part of their relationship based on love? Why or why not?

10. Is Johan acting out of contrition or selflessness when he agrees to adopt Mvelo's baby?

11. Why does Futhi Ntshingila choose to tell this story from different points of view? How do these changing points-of-view in the story strengthen or weaken our understanding of Mvelo's situation and her story?

12. Many women gather to honor Sipho, a man that they loved, after his death even though he had been the source of disease for many of them. What does this imply about the complications and depth of love? What does it imply about the women's feelings toward AIDS itself?

13. Futhi Ntshinglia has written about her interest in how people with so little struggle to maintain normalcy in the face of disaster. In what instances and to what

lengths do the people of *We Kiss Them with Rain* put forth the effort to maintain their normalcy? How has this focus on normalcy helped or hurt the situation?

14. Was there poetic justice in the death of the pastor and will his death allow Mvelo to find some peace?

15. What was your reaction when it was revealed that Mvelo stopped going to the virgin checks because girls had been raped by the men they were intended to trust?

16. Nonceba's grandmother, Mae, felt a pull between her American and African roots that Nonceba also seems to struggle with. Both of these women seemed unsure of where they belonged. What reasons could these women have for such a strong feeling of displacement, and how did this feeling influence where they found themselves throughout the story?

17. *We Kiss Them With Rain* begins with poetry. Some of the poetic images are obvious in the story, but others are more obscure. What ideas exist in the poem but may not be quite as obvious in the text? How does this poem, and the title that comes from it, comment upon the text as a whole and provide perhaps the book's main theme?

OTHER BOOKS FROM CATALYST PRESS

Dark Traces
by Martin Steyn

Sacrificed
by Chanette Paul

The Lion's Binding Oath and Other Stories
by Ahmed Ismail Yusuf

Love Interrupted
by Reneilwe Malatji

OTHER BOOKS FROM STORY PRESS AFRICA

Shaka Rising: A Legend of the Warrior Prince
by Luke Molver